THE HARP AND THE SHADOW

Other books by Alejo Carpentier

The Lost Steps
The Kingdom of This World
Explosion in a Cathedral
War of Time
Reasons of State
The Chase

THE HARP AND THE SHADOW

A NOVEL

ALEJO CARPENTIER

TRANSLATED BY THOMAS CHRISTENSEN AND CAROL CHRISTENSEN

Mercury House, Incorporated
San Francisco

Translation copyright © 1990 by Mercury House, Incorporated. All rights
reserved under International and Pan-American Copyright Conventions.
Originally published in Cuba by Editorial Letras Cubanas, Havana, under the
title *El Arpa y la Sombra,* © Alejo Carpentier, 1979.

Published in the United States by
Mercury House
San Francisco, California

Mercury House and colophon are registered trademarks
of Mercury House, Incorporated

Printed on recycled, acid-free paper
Manufactured in the United States of America

Library of Congress Cataloging-in-Publication Data

Carpentier, Alejo, 1904–1980.
    [Arpa y la sombra. English]
    The harp and the shadow : a novel / by Alejo Carpentier; translated by
Thomas Christensen and Carol Christensen.
        p.   cm.
    ISBN 0–916515–71–0 — ISBN 1–56279–024–2 (pbk.)
    1. Columbus, Christopher—Fiction.   2. Pius IX, Pope, 1792–1878—Fic-
tion. I. Title.
PQ7389.C263A8913   1990
863—dc20   89–13391
                                                              CIP

5   4   3   2   1

For Lilia

This translation is for
Claire and Ellen
Verle and Virginia
Anne

In the sounding of the harp
there are three elements;
the hand, the string, and art.
In man; the body, the soul, and the shadow.

The Golden Legend

CONTENTS

Translators' Preface
Discovering Alejo Carpentier
xi

I ▪ **The Harp**
1

II ▪ **The Hand**
33

III ▪ **The Shadow**
131

DISCOVERING ALEJO CARPENTIER

In a Latin American village, Indian dancers put on painted
wooden masks with fair skin, blue eyes, and blond beards.
They dress in the elaborate Renaissance fashions worn by
Spanish conquistadors expecting to meet the Grand Khan of
the Indies. So begins, in the eternal present of the festival, a
new discovery, a ritual reenactment of the conquest of the
Americas. It is an incongruous but not unusual scene, for in
Latin America the conquest remains a part of daily life, and
signs of it are everywhere: In Mexico, Christian churches rise
on the foundations of Aztec temples; in Central America,
Mayan people praise the hero Tecún Umán, defeater of the
villainous Pedro de Alvarado, and remain largely uncon-
quered; in South America, Inca gold, melted and recast in
the form of saints, adorns the most glorious cathedral
altars.

In North America, by contrast, the conquest is an
abstraction, obscured by Hallmark images of Mayflower
landings and blunderbuss-and-buckle-bedecked fore-
fathers dining thankfully with feathered, moccasined
savages who have stepped from the pages of Lamartine
and Cooper. We have forgotten our origins, rejected and

expunged our native heritage; our imagination only takes hold centuries later, with the pioneer movement west.

"Latin American culture, the culture in which we write, in which we create today, is permeated by the event of the conquest and by the world preceding the conquest, which is not true of North America," Carlos Fuentes once remarked. "In Mexico and the Andean countries and Central America, the Indian world is alive, one way or another. Even if it's only alive in a corrupt religious ceremony, it is there. One can see it, one can visit it. Our language is permeated with Indian words, so it is not something of the past. The past is present in Latin America; the past is past in the United States."

It is not surprising then that for us Christopher Columbus is little more than a name, a list of ships, and a date recited by schoolchildren. Of the man himself we know almost nothing. Yet his discovery of our lands determined to a large degree the course of our history. "It is in fact the conquest of America that heralds and establishes our present identity," Tzvetan Todorov writes in *The Conquest of America*. And he adds, "We are all the direct descendants of Columbus." (Likewise, all American translators—that abject lot!—are descendants of our mother La Malinche, Cortés's informer, the famous whore and traitor.)

Because the discovery and conquest are experienced almost as contemporary events by Latin Americans, they have been the most astute interpreters of those events. Among modern novelists, Miguel Ángel Asturias and Fuentes have produced notable works on the theme, and Gabriel García Márquez has been strongly influenced by the fabulous chronicles of the Spanish explorers; recently, the Brazilian João Ubaldo Ribeiro traced consequences of the conquest down to the present in his sweeping novel *An Invincible Memory,* while in Argentina Abel Posse has published an extraordinary new novel based on the Columbus story, *The Dogs of Paradise.* But *The Harp and the Shadow* remains the prototype (no doubt this is why Eduardo

Galeano, in *The Memory of Fire,* his interpretive history of the Americas, quotes from it at the beginning of his account).

The encounter of the Old and New Worlds, the give and take of colliding cultures and traditions, has been a recurring theme in Carpentier's work. In *The Lost Steps,* for example, a Spanish American musicologist returns from Europe to make a visit to one of the sources of native American culture, traveling up the Orinoco River to dwell with an Indian tribe. In *Explosion in a Cathedral,* the spirit of the French Revolution arrives in the New World in the company of one of its more gruesome symbols, the guillotine, where it is reshaped by a tangle of indigenous secret societies, voodoo, and other local traditions. And in another historical novel, *The Kingdom of This World,* the nineteenth-century Haitian ruler Henri Christophe finds himself torn between French and Afro-Caribbean cultures.

But it is in Columbus's voyages that we find the quintessential encounter of the self with the Other, an other that is completely unknown and unknowable, unfathomable and uninterpretable. In this postlapsarian confrontation, language itself has no referents — the other becomes a mirror to the self, harshly exposing the flaws that lie at the foundation of our American culture. In Columbus's fall, we sinned all.

Mexican historian Edmundo O'Gorman proposes in *The Invention of America* that America was not discovered but invented. The invention begins with Columbus. Discovering unknown peoples, Columbus shapes them by turns into Edenic innocents, sickly Moors, and villainous cannibals — even the name he gives them, "Indians," is based on a fundamental misconception (or preconception). New World fruits, birds, trees, people — Columbus lacks the words to understand or to convey most of what he has discovered; in this sense he has failed to discover anything. "I say that the blue mountains I can see in the distance are like those of Sicily, though they are nothing like those of Sicily. I say the grass is as tall as that of

Andalusia in April and May, though there is nothing here that is anything like Andalusia. I say nightingales are singing when I hear twittering little gray birds with long black beaks that are more like sparrows. I allude to the fields of Castile, here where not a single thing recalls the fields of Castile. I have seen no spice trees, and I suggest that there may be spices here. . . ."

Instead of an unspoiled tropical paradise, Columbus sees, finally, nothing but a monstrous mine of gold, which exists only in his imagination. In desperation, unable to produce gold from this mine, he transfers its wholly imaginary value to the human resources he has found, balancing his mental ledgers by means of the institution of slavery and firmly planting greed, deceit, and oppression in the fertile ground of our hemisphere. And so begins our modern history, which, in 1992, will celebrate its first half millennium.

I

THE HARP

Praise him with trumpet sound;

Praise him with lute and harp!

Psalm 150

They turned their backs on the confessional altar with its eighty-seven candles, which had flickered more than once that morning, the glass holders vibrating as the swelling voices of the pontifical choir sang out a triumphant Te Deum; they softly closed the monumental doors of the basilica behind them as they emerged from its brilliant light into the chapel of the Holy Sacrament, which was suffused with twilight shadows; and then they lowered the sedan chair, transferring it from their shoulders to their hands and holding it suspended a few inches from the floor. The *flabelli* planted the shafts of the massive feathered fans in their racks, and the red-robed porters began their slow walk, bending their knees to pass through the low-linteled doorways, carrying His Holiness through the innumerable rooms that still separated him from his private chambers. On both sides of the long, long passage that led past rooms and galleries, they passed muted oils, retables darkened by time, faded tapestries; there a person looking with an outsider's curiosity would have seen mythological allegories, triumphs of the Faith, beatific faces lifted in prayer, or incidents from the lives of the saints. Rather fatigued, his Papal Holiness was barely conscious of the dignitaries of his retinue exiting the procession by rank and category, disappearing through their various doors according to the strict protocol of the ceremony. The first to vanish were the pairs of cardinals, *de cappa magna,* their trains carefully carried by clergymen; after them, the bishops, removing their resplendent miters; next, the canons, the chaplains, the apostolic prothonotaries, the heads of congregations, the prelates of the private bedchamber, the military officers, the monsignor majordomo and the monsignor camerlengo: so that when the procession had nearly reached the rooms whose windows faced the Court of Saint Damasus, the pomp of gold and violet and garnet, of moiré, silk, and lace, gave way to the less showy uniforms of domestics, doorkeepers, and *bussolanti*. At last the sedan chair was lowered to the floor near His Holiness's modest worktable; then, after the chair had been freed of its august cargo, the porters raised it back up and retired with repeated reverences. Once he was seated in an armchair that gave him a reassuring feeling of stability, the pope requested an orgeat drink from Sor Crescencia, who was responsible for his refreshments, and then dismissed her with a gesture that included his valets as well; he listened to the shutting of the door — the final door — that separated him from the glittering, pulsing world of the princes of the church, the palatine prelates, dignitaries, and patriarchs whose staffs and capes became confused — in swirling clouds of incense raised by the zealous censer-bearers — with the cloaks and swords of the uniformed Ceramistas, Royal Guards, and Swiss Guards, who were magnificent in their silver armor, ancient halberds, helmets *allo condottiero*, and orange-and-blue-striped uniforms: colors permanently assigned them by the brush of Michelangelo, whose work and memory are inextricably linked with the sumptuous existence of the basilica.

It was hot. Because all the windows facing the Court of Saint Damasus — except his, of course — had been walled up to prevent indiscreet glances from prying into the pontiff's private domain, an absolute silence reigned there; the place was so free from the sounds of urban activity, the passage of carriages and the noises of workmen, that when the echo of some faraway bell drifted in, it sounded like distant music evoking an otherworldly Rome. The Vicar of the Lord could identify some bells by their sounds, borne to him on the breeze. This light one, reverberating in a narrow range, was from the baroque Church of Jesus; that nearer one, majestic and deliberate, was from Santa

Maria Maggiore; another one, solemn and intense, was from Santa Maria sopra Minerva, which housed in its interior, within a forest of incarnate marble, the human vestiges of Katherine of Siena, the fiery, energetic nun who had been an impassioned defender of his predecessor, Urban VI; he himself had honored that irascible protagonist of the Western Schism five years before by publishing the combative *Syllabus* — he didn't sign it, but everyone knew that the text derived from his sermons, homilies, encyclicals, and pastoral letters — in which he used clear, rigorous Latin prose to excoriate *les pestes* of the modern period, socialism and communism, clandestine societies (that is, the Freemasons), "biblical societies" (warning to the United States): all the liberal-clerical groups assailing the ear in those days. The *Syllabus* caused such an uproar that Napoleon III, who had never been accused of liberalism, tried to prevent its distribution in France, where the middle clergy were astonished by such intransigence, since they had already criticized the preparatory encyclical, *Cuanta Cura,* as excessively intolerant and extreme; oh, but its condemnation of religious liberalism was very mild compared to Pope Urban's almost biblical opprobrium, which was supported so fiercely by the Sienese nun — he was reminded of her for the second time that day by the tolling of the bell of Santa Maria sopra Minerva! The *Syllabus* had slowly matured in his thoughts after he had journeyed to the Americas and observed the power of spreading philosophical and political ideas that were oblivious to the boundaries of seas and mountains. He had observed their power in Buenos Aires and all along the Andean cordillera during the trip — so long ago, so rich in useful lessons — that he had undertaken despite the sweet, sad protests of his saintly mother, Countess Antonia Catarina Solazzi, the exemplary spouse of his strict, proud, and righteous father, Count Girolamo Mastaï-Ferretti, so severe, so imposing; he remembered how as a frail and sickly boy he had listened to his father's boasting about the coveted gonfalons of Sinigaglia . . . Now, in the peace following the pomp and splendor of the morning's ceremonies, the distant chorus of Roman cowbells resonated with the crystalline syllables of Sinigaglia, bringing back memories of the times between the tolling of the church bells, when he danced hand in hand in the courtyard of the vast manorial house with his older sisters, who had such lovely names — Maria Virginia, Maria Isabella, Maria Tecla, Maria Olimpia, Catarina Juditta — and fresh, gay voices whose tones he could almost hear, reminding him of those other girls' voices, joined in simple carols at the beginning of a rainy Christmas season in the distant, so distant and yet so vividly remembered, city of Santiago, Chile:

> *Tonight is Christmas Eve*
> *Not a night to shut your eyes*
> *For the Virgin is with child*
> *And at midnight He will arrive*

But, suddenly, the great voice of Santa Maria sopra Minerva wrenched him from these reflections, which were perhaps too frivolous for a day when he had resolved to make an important decision, despite his weariness after the long ceremony that had flooded Saint Peter's Basilica with light. Between an ornamental pyx attributed to Benvenuto Cellini and an ancient rock-crystal thurible in the form of the *Ictus* of the Christian primitives lay the docket — the famous petition! — that had been awaiting his decision for a year. No one had been so disrespectful as to prod him, but certainly the very venerable Cardinal of Bordeaux, the Metropolitan of the Diocese of the Antilles, his Eminence the Cardinal Archbishop of Burgos, the Very Illustrious Archbishop of Mexico, as well as the six hundred and some bishops who had affixed their signatures to the document, must have waited for his resolution impatiently. He opened the docket full of large papers covered with wax seals, tied in folios with ribbons of red satin, and he read for the twentieth time the Postulation for the

Holy Congregation of Rites, which began with the well-turned phrase: *Post hominum salutem, ab Incarnato Dei Verbo, Domino Nostro Jesu Cristo, feliciter instauratam, nullum profecto eventum extitit aut praeclarius, aut utilius incredibili ausu Januensis nautae Christophori Columbi, qui omnium primus inexplorata horrentiaque Oceani aequora pertransiens, ignotum Mundum detexit, et ita porro terrarum mariumque tractus Evangelicae fidei propagationi duplicavit.* . . . The Primate of Bordeaux had put it well: Christopher Columbus's discovery of the New World was the greatest event witnessed by man since the world had received the Christian faith; thanks to that unparalleled accomplishment, *the extent of known lands and seas to which the word of the Gospels could be carried had been doubled.* . . . And on a separate page attached to the respectful petition there was a brief message to the Holy Congregation of Rites, which awaited only the pope's signature to set in motion the intricate process of the beatification of the Grand Admiral of Ferdinand and Isabella. His Holiness took the pen, but his hand hovered uncertainly over the page, rendered powerless once again by the implications of each word. This happened every time he resolved to trace the decisive rubric at the foot of the document. And all because one paragraph contained an underscored sentence that always made him hesitate: . . . *pro introductione illius causae exceptionali ordine.* Because the postulation required an *exceptional procedure,* the Supreme Pontiff hesitated one more time. Certainly the Vatican annals contained no precedents for the beatification—the first step toward canonization—of the Discoverer of America: the petition lacked certain biographical documentation necessary to the granting of an aureole, according to the canon. According to the wise and impartial Bollandists who were invited to offer opinions, this deficiency would certainly be utilized by the Devil's Advocate, that subtle and intimidating Minister of the Republic of the Inferno . . . He, Pius IX, had been Archbishop of Spoleto, Bishop of Emilia, and a cardinal before being elected to the

Throne of Saint Peter; in 1851, when he had occupied that throne for only five years, he had commissioned a French historian, Count Roselly de Lorgues, to write a *Biography of Christopher Columbus,* which the pope had read and pondered repeatedly, since it seemed invaluable for any decision about the canonization of the Discoverer of the New World. The Catholic historian was an ardent admirer of his subject, so he had emphasized the virtues that made the famous Genoan mariner such an important figure, worthy of a prominent place in the litany of saints and in the churches — hundreds, thousands of churches — where people would venerate his image, an image as yet rather imprecise, since there were no portraits of him — wasn't that often the case with saints? — but soon to acquire corporeality and character, thanks to the pioneering efforts of an inspired painter who endowed him with all the power and expression that Bronzino, Cesar Borgia's portrait painter, had given the famous mariner Andrea Doria in an exceptionally beautiful oil painting. Columbus's canonization had obsessed Mastaï ever since his return from America, when he was a young canon, never dreaming that one day he would occupy the throne in Saint Peter's Basilica. It was necessary to make a saint of Christopher Columbus for many reasons, reasons of faith as much as of politics — and ever since he had published the *Syllabus,* it had been apparent that he, Pius IX, did not disdain political action, political action inspired by the politics of God, as anyone who had studied Saint Augustine understood. To sign the decree before him would be a gesture that would stand as one of the momentous decisions of his papacy . . . Again he started to dip his pen in the ink, and yet again he held the pen suspended above the page. He wavered anew, this summer afternoon while the bells of Rome joined as one in the ringing of the angelus.

When Mastaï was a child, Sinigaglia was already in decline; no longer a city with lively bazaars and a busy port welcoming ships from all over the Mediterranean and the Adriatic, it had been absorbed by rich, proud, wicked Trieste, whose prosperity was in danger of ruining its pitiful neighbor, once the favorite of Greek navigators. And those were especially difficult times: Bonaparte had thrown the world into turmoil with his devastating Italian campaign, occupying Ferrara and Bologna, taking over Romana and Ancona, humiliating the Church, despoiling the Pontifical States, incarcerating cardinals, occupying Rome itself; he had even carried his insolence as far as arresting the pope and taking prized antiquities from Christian monasteries to exhibit in Paris—the height of mockery!—between Osiris and Anubis, falcons and crocodiles, from a museum of Egyptian artifacts . . . Times were hard. And so the fortunes of the manor of the counts of Mastaï-Ferretti had been reduced. There was no concealing the deterioration of the family portraits, the faded tapestries, the fly-specked engravings, the high sideboards and dull curtains, the increasing damage to the walls, which were covered with ever-widening stains—dark and ugly—as more leaks appeared with every passing day. The old wooden floors were starting to buckle from moisture, the fine finished woodwork was coming unglued, the marquetry was beginning to fall apart. Every week, two or three more strings on the aged pianoforte were broken, and certain notes, missing from the yellowing keyboard, had not sounded for several months; yet Maria Virginia and Maria Olimpia overlooked their silence and persisted in playing pieces for two or four hands—sonatinas by Muzio Clementi, compositions by Father Martini, or *Nocturnes*—a lovely novelty—by an Englishman named Field. The impressive family colors were all that gave the look of a great lord to Count Mastaï-Ferretti; after attending public ceremonies he would come back to a house whose cupboards were bare and change into a frock coat that had been darned and redarned by two self-sacrificing maidservants who had stayed on, collecting wages one year and not the next. For the most part, the countess put a good face on her bad fortune; she kept up appearances with her usual dignity, observing a mourning period for imaginary relatives who had died in always distant cities in order to justify the constant wearing of a pair of black dresses that were only a little out of style, and avoiding public scrutiny by attending the early service at the church of Las Servitas, accompanied by her younger son, Giovanni Maria, to petition the Madonna Addolorata to assist the troubled northern states and relieve their distress and suffering. In short, they led an existence of proud penury in ruined palaces, as did so many Italian families of that period. Pride and misery—an escutcheon on the door and no faggots for the fireplace, a breast decorated with the Maltese cross and a belly full of hunger—the same pride and misery the young Mastaï, who was studying Castilian, found reflected in the novels of the Spanish picaresque; but he soon abandoned those frivolous readings, immersed himself in the meandering concepts of Gracián, and then moved on to study the *Spiritual Exercises* of Saint Ignatius, where he learned meditation and practice that were more beneficial to his soul: he learned to focus his mind—or oration—on a previously selected image, to concentrate on "local composition," and avoid the impulsive flights of imagination that were his eternal downfall, allowing foreign themes to intrude on the principal subject.

The world had been turned upside down. Freemasonry was taking hold everywhere. It had been barely forty years—and what were forty years in the course of history?—since the deaths of Voltaire and Rousseau, those masters of impious and wanton philosophies. Less than thirty years before, a most Christian king had been guillotined without a word of protest from a godless, republican mob, to the tattoo of drums sporting the red and blue of the revolutionary struggle . . . Indecisive about his future after a strange combination of studies that included teleology, civil law, Castilian, French, and an elevated Latin based on the study of Virgil, Horace, and even Ovid—

nothing particularly practical — he began to frequent a brilliant Roman society that welcomed him because of his name, unaware that what the young man who rarely had the money for a tavern meal appreciated most about the receptions — more than the décolletage of the beautiful women, more than the balls where the licentious novelty of the waltz had been introduced, more than the concerts given by famous musicians in splendid mansions — was the call of the majordomo to the candelabra-lit dining room where dishes abundant enough to sate his deprived appetite were served up on silver trays. But one day, after an unfortunate amorous incident, the young Giovanni Maria traded the wine of gold-edged crystal carafes for the waters of the cloistral springs, and the exquisitely prepared game hens of the palace kitchens for the chick-peas, cabbages, and porridge of the refectories. He had resolved to serve the Church, and he quickly entered the Third Order of Saint Francis. Ordained a priest, he was distinguished by the ardor and eloquence of his sermons. But he knew that a long and difficult road lay ahead of him, with little hope of ascending to the upper reaches of the church hierarchy because his family was so isolated and his relatives so few, but especially because the times were confused and turbulent. Since the former social equilibrium — which may not always have been satisfactory but was at least an equilibrium — had been destroyed by the dangerous iconoclasms of the French Revolution, Christianity had become divided, dismembered, weaker than ever before, as it was forced to face the growing and almost universal assault of new ideas, theories, and doctrines, each of them tending in one way or another to the elaboration of dangerous utopian visions . . . And all was darkness, humility, and resignation in his life, when a miracle occurred: Monsignor Giovanni Muzzi, Archbishop of Philippopolis, in Macedonia — and a descendent of Alexander the Great — was named apostolic delegate to Chile, an extremely delicate mission for which he requested Mastaï's assistance.

Muzzi had never met the prelate he selected on an abbé friend's recommendation, but he thought the cultivated young canon might be useful, especially since he knew Castilian. And so the future pope went from a hospice where he held a modest post as protector of orphans to the enviable position of Envoy to the New World — that New World whose very name flooded his senses with a marvelous scent of adventure, just as his long robes filled him with a sense of his missionary vocation — a vocation he may well have owed to his knowledge of the missionary work of the disciples of Saint Ignatius in China, the Far East, the Philippines, and Paraguay. Suddenly he envisioned a missionary role for himself: he was conscious that times had changed, that politics had become increasingly important in the new century, but he did not imitate the Jesuits (as described by Voltaire in a novel that had been widely read — even translated into Castilian by the renegade abbé Marchena), but rather began to explore the full range of subjects relevant to a field in which one had to act with cleverness, tact, and discretion.

From the beginning he found one fact especially intriguing. Pope Pius VII had received the request to send an apostolic mission to Chile from Bernardo O'Higgins, who was Director General, head of the Chilean government. O'Higgins had liberated Chile from Spanish colonial rule, Mastaï knew that much, but he did not understand why O'Higgins had appealed to the Vatican luminaries to reorganize the Chilean Church. Rome, in those confused, chaotic times, was haven and sanctuary for intriguers of every stripe, conspirators and sacripants, cloaked Carbonari, secularized monks, penitent renegade priests, Voltairean ex-curates who had returned to the flock, informers and denouncers, and — these last were everywhere — deserters from the Lodges, ready and willing to sell the secrets of freemasonry for thirty denarii. Mastaï had talked to one of these deserters, an ex-cavalier Kadosh of the Elevated Lodges of Cádiz, which were affiliated with the Great American Union of London, founded

by Francisco de Miranda, and now boasting branches in Buenos Aires, Mendoza, and Santiago. And—according to the
informer—O'Higgins was quite friendly with a formidable
Venezuelan, mentor of Simón Bolívar and general of the French
Revolution, whose worldly exploits would make a fantastic
adventure novel; they even say—"deliver me, God, from impure
thoughts," thought Mastaï—that he slept with Catherine the
Great, when "her lover Potemkin, worn out by the excessive
ardors of the sovereign, decided that the handsome hot-blooded
Creole might be able to satisfy the outrageous appetites of the
Russian empress, who may have been getting on in years, if you
know what I mean, but was still tremendously fond of . . ."
"Enough, enough, enough," said Mastaï to his informer. "Let's
talk about something more serious . . . over a little more wine."
The renegade wet his whistle, praising the quality of a red wine
so crude that only his perennial thirst enabled him to appreciate
it, and resumed his account. In their secret language, the Freemasons called Spain "The Columns of Hercules." And the
Lodges of Cádiz held a "Secret Commission" that concerned
itself almost exclusively with promoting political unrest in the
Hispanic world. Every member of that commission knew that
while he was in London Miranda had dictated a paper, "Advice
from an Old South American to a Young Patriot Returning to
His Homeland from England," which contained such thoughts
as *Never trust anyone over forty, unless he is an avid reader. Youth is the
age of passionate, generous sentiments. Among your peers you will find
many who are ready to listen and easy to convince.* ("Evidently this
Miranda, like Gracián, is suspicious of *the horrors and honors of old
age,* and places his confidence in *the enchanted palace of youth,*"
reflected Mastaï . . .) The prominent Freemason had also written: *It is a mistake to think that any man who wears a tonsure or
occupies the seat of a canon is an intolerant fanatic and an inexorable
enemy of the rights of man.* "I am starting to understand this
Bernardo O'Higgins," said Mastaï, after making the fugitive

from the Cádiz Lodges repeat the paragraph three times. It was clear to him now: O'Higgins knew that the Spanish, whatever their ideals, dreamt of reestablishing authority over their waning colonial empire in America; they were fighting fiercely to win decisive battles on the western rim of the continent before beginning a true war of reconquest to quash the independent governments that had recently been established elsewhere — and they would stop at nothing to accomplish that end. O'Higgins was aware that the Church could not rid itself overnight of the governments — by viceroys or captain generals — that it had woken up to one morning, and he knew that the South American churches had always been subject to the Spanish episcopacy rather than having to render obedience to Rome; therefore — since any Spanish priest could be an ally of the potential invaders — the liberator of Chile wanted to place his country's churches under the influence of the *ex metropoli,* making them subject to the supreme authority of the Vatican, which was weaker than ever politically, able to accomplish little outside the ecclesiastical sphere in lands across the sea. Thus a vengeful clergy, contentious and conservative, were neutralized by being placed under the direct charge of the Vicar of the Lord on Earth — and what's more they could not complain about it! A masterstroke, however you looked at it! . . . The young Mastaï felt a growing admiration for this Bernardo O'Higgins. He was eager to cross the ocean, despite the anxious protests of his sainted mother, the countess — she begged him from her sagging mansion in Sinigaglia to use his weak health as an excuse to avoid the exhausting voyage across the violent ocean that had wrecked so many ships. "The same sea crossed by Christopher Columbus," thought the canon as the great journey drew near and he nostalgically recalled the tranquillity of his family life, thinking with special tenderness of Maria Tecla, his favorite sister, whom he had sometimes surprised when their parents were out, singing softly, as if in a dream (oh, most trifling, most innocent of sins!), a French romance that had appeared in an album of works by Father Martini, the great Franciscan, composer of so many masses and oratorios:

Plaisir d'amour
ne dure qu'un moment.
Chagrin d'amour
dure toute la vie.

Despite appeals to caution and prudence, the young canon anxiously awaited the day of departure. And even more so since recent events seemed to conspire against the enterprise: the death of the humiliated pope who had been forced by the insolent Corsican to sanction the mockery of his imperial investiture with a crown placed, solemnly, on the head of a mulatta from Martinique; the election of Leo XII after a conclave that dragged on for twenty-six days; a series of intrigues by the Spanish consul, whose spies had informed him of the object of the apostolic mission; foul winds, plots, gossip, letters flying back and forth, replies that were less than reassuring. But, at last—at last!—on the fifth of October, 1823, the ship *Héloise* ("Better Abelard's Héloise than Rousseau's," mused Mastaï) raised its anchors and set sail for the New World. With him on the voyage: the Delegate Giovanni Muzzi, his personal secretary Don Salustio, the Dominican Raimundo Arce, and the Archdeacon Cienfuegos, plenipotentiary minister from Chile—by recent appointment of O'Higgins—to the Holy See.

The vessel departed from Genoa. It had been a native of Genoa who launched the extraordinary adventure that gave man a consummate vision of his world, opening the way for Copernicus and his explorations of the infinite. The way to America, the way to Santiago, *campus stellae*—in reality the way to the other stars: the initial human passage to the multiplicity of sidereal immensities.

. . . Exasperating as the young canon had found the prolonged delay in Genoa, it had been rich in discovery for him: he had marveled with every step at the splendor of the sober city of the Dorias—that golden, sonorous name—full of the memory of Andrea, the famous admiral who was depicted in allegorical paintings bare chested, curly bearded, emblematic trident in hand, like a real, living, contemporary image of Poseidon. The young man had stood for a long time before the house of Branca Doria, meditating on that most magnificent of Genoan murderers, encountered by Dante in the ninth circle of hell where his soul suffered its punishment even as his body, possessed by a devil, *appeared, still living, above*. Near the church of San Mateo, the mansion built by Martino Doria for Lamba Doria had withstood the passage of the centuries, its construction every bit as solid as the lineage of its owners; as solid as the high, beautiful mansion of Domenicaccio Doria and that of Constantino Doria, which had, finally, been inhabited by Andrea—everyone here seems to be named Doria!—the prodigious mariner who won a hundred victories over the Turks . . . And even now, as the *Héloise* entered the muddy waters of the Rio de la Plata, Mastaï could not forget the magnificent port he had left behind, the pomp of the city with its red palaces and its white palaces, its stained glass, its balustrades, columned domes, and slender campaniles. Montevideo was quite a contrast: entering its bay was like entering a vast stable; there were no imposing or beautiful buildings here, they were all rustic, like outbuildings on a farm; and not only that but horses and livestock had an importance in the life of Montevideo that they had not had in Europe since Merovingian times. Buenos Aires didn't even have a port, just a miserable bay—you had to travel to the city in a horse-drawn cart, escorted by men on horseback, surrounded by a stench of horses, a smell of raw leather, and a cacophony of neighing—it was inescapable, the horse's presence was forced on the traveler as soon as he set foot on this continent and as long as he stayed on its ground. The city that had been without a bishop for so long welcomed the apostolic mission by the light of lanterns carried by its citizens. Mastaï's first impression was not favorable. The streets were straight enough, as if they had been laid out in a line, but they were too full of churned-up mud, which seemed to have been dampened, then tamped down, dampened, then tamped down, kneaded and turned, by the hooves of horses, by the wheels of oxcarts, by the oxen spurred on by goads. There were black people, many black people in the city, serving in lowly jobs and modest trades, as street vendors singing the praise of the fat cabbages and fresh carrots under their rectangular umbrellas, or as servants in comfortable homes; these servants looked so respectable compared to the black workers wearing blood-splotched garments who carried guts from the slaughterhouse — which seemed so important in the life of Buenos Aires that Mastaï finally began to wonder whether the cult of steaks, fillets, ribs, loins, chops — what those who had studied English had started to call *bife* — had not turned the slaughterhouse into a more important building than the cathedral or the parish church of San Nicolás, or La Concepción, Montserrat, or La Piedad. There was too strong a stink of leatherworks, tanneries, cattle and livestock, of hides and curing, hung beef and jerky, of sweat off the flanks of horses and their riders, of dung and manure, in that overseas city whose citizens were dancing in convents and stores and brothels to *"El Refalosa"* and *"Cuándo, Mi Vida, Cuándo?"* — dances that were the rage in those days, all over the American continent, even though, outside the walls, the drums of mestizos and blacks were beginning a clamorous assault, beating out the rhythms of the "tango," as it was called here. But alongside these groups there was a thriving aristocracy, who enjoyed the most luxurious and refined existence, who wore the latest Paris and London fashions and staged dazzling balls where the latest European dance music could be heard; and, during religious festivals, there were always many pretty Creole girls singing Pergolesi's *Stabat Mater* to please the young canon. But, unfortunately, the overseas fashions in clothing, entertainment, and culture never traveled alone. They carried with them the "dangerous passion of thinking," and Mastaï knew that what made it a "dangerous passion" was the urge to seek truths and verities, or new possibilities, where there were only ashes and shadows, the dark night of the soul. Certain ideas had crossed the wide ocean with the writings of Voltaire and Rousseau — which the young canon argued against indirectly, calling them *sclerotic* and *outmoded,* denying all currency to books that were already more than half a century old. But those books had influenced many people for whom even the French Revolution, viewed from a distance, had not been a failure. And the proof was that the apostolic mission's visit to Buenos Aires was viewed with considerable antipathy by the government minister Bernardino Rivadavia. A liberal and almost certainly a Freemason, he informed Archbishop Muzzi that they would not be allowed to administer confirmation in the city, instructing them to continue their journey at once — and not only that but he tried to spoil their journey in advance, insinuating that the emissaries of the Roman Church might not be received in Chile quite as warmly as they imagined.

Thus, in mid-January, 1824, the clergymen took to the road in two wide coaches, followed by a slow cart piled up with trunks, bags, and supplies — in addition to beds and essential cooking utensils that were hard to come by in the inns where they changed horses and where they often had to sleep for want of any better accommodations. Amply supplied by sympathetic citizens, who were incensed by the impiety and incivility of Rivadavia — who had not offered any official aid to the mission — the travelers carried abundant stores of food: grains, potatoes, mutton, salt pork, garlic and onions, lemons to take the place of the tainted vinegar of the country's interior, as well as many casks of wine, *aguardiente,* and *mistela.* "And they say that prelates dine on nothing but fillet of trout and lark pastries!" commented Giovanni Muzzi, laughing. Mastaï said little but observed much. The country was unbearably monotonous, but its grand scale captured his attention. He had never seen anything like the pampas, these plains that seemed endless; no matter how far the travelers went, they always seemed to be surrounded by an unvarying vista — the pampas gave the traveler the impression of not moving, never advancing on his course, no matter how hard he drove his team. The vastness of the pampas — their perfect embodiment of the infinite, confronting man with an image of the limitless — made Mastaï think of a mystical vision, an allegory in which man is placed in a corridor without beginning or end and spends years trying, through science and learning, to push back the enclosing walls that limit his vision; gradually he succeeds, gradually he makes them recede, but no matter how far he pushes them, he can never manage to destroy them or alter their appearance or learn what hides behind them . . . As he crossed the pampas, Mastaï spent day after day immersed in himself, lost in a vivid dream — sometimes disturbed by the shouts of a band galloping in a riot of bolas — from which he was finally shaken awake by the reappearance of scenes that caused this land to resemble the one across the sea: certain features of the landscape, such as arroyos and marshes, familiar plants and animals, houses like the ones back home, no longer dwarfed by the vastness of nature. But soon the horizontal infinity was transformed into a vertical infinity, that of the Andes. Compared to these incredible cliffs rising up from the earth, their summits hidden in the clouds — seemingly inaccessible (of course, they had only reached the first buttresses) — the Dolomite Mountains, which he had known as a youth, seemed no more than parks for strolls and picnics; the gigantic scale of America was so striking that the continent had already begun to seem unreal to him even though the people who lived in it usually appeared uncivilized, brutal, and mean. Such a landscape could not produce men who were otherwise — he thought — but in the future, when the continent matures and begins to be aware of its own possibilities, who could predict what kind of men, what promises, what ideas would emerge. Still everything he had seen up to now "lacked balance," as the tasters of fine wines would put it.

And then began a slow and arduous ascent: to the peaks that divided the map, creating the rivers and their routes, forming paths along the edges of precipices or through ravines where thundering torrents crashed down from the crests of invisible snowy summits, amid the howling of snowstorms and the screeching of windstorms; and still higher up, to the desolation of high plateaus, and the aridity of punas, and the fear of heights, and the depth of the chasms, and the stupor induced by the granite immensities, the multitude of crags and peaks, the black slabs lined up like penitents in a procession, the schist staircases, and an illusory vision of ruined cities constructed of rocks so old, so ancient, that shards of minerals had been stripped from them, exposing the naked, polished skeleton of the planet. And climbing from one summit to the next, and then to a third, and to a fourth, until they reached the pinnacle, the seventh heaven, as they called it, before beginning the descent to the valleys of Chile, where the vegetation achieved a greater verdure than above, among the lichens nourished by the clouds. The trail was almost impassable. A recent earthquake had caused a landslide that spilled debris on the bleak, patchy grasses . . . And happy to be returning at last to the world of trees and cultivated fields — after a journey that had begun nine months before in Genoa — the apostolic mission arrived at Santiago, Chile. "We have finally been delivered," said Mastaï, with relief, "from an extremely difficult labor!"

he young canon saw so many churches and convents in the city of Santiago that he decided it resembled certain Italian villages, which had twenty belfries for every hundred roofs. If Buenos Aires smelled of hides and tanneries and harnesses—and (why deny it?) of horse shit—here one constantly inhaled clouds of incense rising from the walls and cloisters of Santo Domingo, San Antonio, San Francisco, Las Recoletas, Las Clarisas, Los Agustinos, La Compañía, San Diego, and La Veracruz, not to mention the crowded convent that occupied the main square. Just as Mastaï was congratulating himself on beginning a splendid career as an auditor in such a propitious setting, the uneasy travelers were presented with a new setback: there had been a revolt two months before against Bernardo O'Higgins, Chile's Director, the man who had asked Monsignor Muzzi to bring his mission to the country, through the intermediary of his ambassador Cienfuegos; O'Higgins, hero of the hard-fought and glorious war of independence, had been overthrown by his right-hand man, Ramón Freire, Lieutenant General of the Armed Forces of Chile. And Freire was not in the capital; military matters had called him to the distant island of Chiloé . . . ("The true generals, who rule by the sword, are not yet dead, and generals of the sheath have already begun to emerge," thought the young ecclesiastic.) All prior commitments were nullified. No one knew what Freire's policy would be. And so began an exasperating period of waiting, during which Mastaï wrote a letter that revealed how frustrated he was by this turn of events: *The present American governments are convulsive governments as a result of the continual changes to which they are subjected.* ("Without wishing to be, I became the Pale Angel of Vatican Sorrows," murmured His Holiness Pius IX—once an obscure canon—when he reread a copy of the letter he had preserved for so many years, a letter that presaged so many dramatic developments.) But Mastaï did not succumb to this first serious blow to his ambition. As he waited to begin his work, he cultivated the friendships that the cordial and cultured people of Santiago were quick to offer him. He was a frequent visitor to the Cotapos household; the young ladies there were fond of music and helped him pass his hours of waiting—in deference to his tonsure, they played him Pergolesi's *Stabat Mater*. ("It is curious," thought Mastaï, "that with a single melody a composer who died at twenty-six achieved greater fame than the aged Palestrina did with his enormous body of work, written over the course of a long life.") "His opera *La Serva Padrona* is equally popular here," said the Cotapos ladies, "and we know some parts of it. But the plot would shock Your Reverence by its daring." Mastaï acknowledged their scruples with an indulgent but somewhat hypocritical smile, since he recalled that he and his sister Maria Tecla had passed one extremely pleasant afternoon in Sinigaglia softly singing the two principal parts of that delightful entertainment (the third part was silent) from sheet music propped up on the battered family piano. From the Chilean girls he learned some of the carols that brightened the city—which they said was melancholy and gray enough the rest of the time—once a year, at Christmas. One of these carols, quite a popular melody, enchanted him with its fresh if rather foolish ingenuousness:

> *Señora Doña María*
> *I have come from far away*
> *To bring your little one*
> *Some bunnies*

When Holy Week arrived, the new auditor was amazed at the
medieval drama of the somber procession of penitents filing
through the central streets of the city, celebrating the agony of
Our Lord on Good Friday: each barefoot man was wearing a
long white tunic and a crown of thorns, carrying a heavy
wooden cross and a whip, and each was furiously flagellating his
shoulders . . . The religious fervor in this country could not
help but further the goals of the apostolic mission, thought
Mastaï. But at the same time he was aware that this city, just like
Buenos Aires, had seen the insidious incursion of the so-called
new ideas. Watching the flagellants bloody the ground with
their expiatory worship were some dandified young heathens —
"young Turks," they were called by the natives — who wanted to
see Mastaï squirm: they told him that freedom of the press
would soon be reestablished — it had been suspended during the
recent war — and that Freire had a secret plan to secularize the
Chilean clergy. As Mastaï awaited developments, he adopted a
new tactic to deal with the people who dared to express liberal
sentiments in his presence: a tactic that consisted of pretending
to be more liberal than the liberals themselves. Following a
strategy he had learned from the Jesuits, he praised Voltaire and
Rousseau as extraordinarily talented men — he could not hold to
their views, of course, since he was a priest — but then went on to
remind his listeners, with subtle perfidy, that those philosophers
belonged to a generation whose outmoded notions had been
supplanted by a new generation of thinkers: it was time to get in
step, to adopt the rhythm of the new era, time to put aside those
moth-eaten texts, those old ideas history had already discredited, time to adopt a "new philosophy." And the French
Revolution? Time had passed it by; it had failed in its most
fundamental principles — which were discussed entirely too
much on this continent, when nobody remembered them anymore in Europe. "Sclerosis, senectitude, superannuation — people from another century," he said, describing the *Social Contract*

and the Encyclopedists. "Utopian zeal that accomplished nothing, unfulfilled promises, betrayed ideals . . .

"It could have been great," he said, "but it never lived up to its originators' dreams," speaking of the French Revolution. "I am only a priest, whom you might imagine would be hemmed in by dogma and old-fashioned ways of thinking, but even I know these things." No, no, no. Liberalism is not what you young men think it is, not anymore. Today there is a new kind of liberalism: a liberalism — how shall I put it? — situated to the left of the left — bearing in mind that in the convention hall, the Jacobins always occupied the leftmost rows. "Should we be more Jacobin than the Jacobins?" they asked him. "It is possible that these times call for a new way of being a Jacobin," responded the future author of the *Syllabus,* whose knack for manipulating his opponents' arguments allowed him to ascend to the papacy with a reputation as an extremely liberal friend of progress.

In the months that followed, the delegates were filled with hope as well as with impatience and irritation, anguish and agitation, depression and dismay, in the face of Freire's hostile cunning; elevated to the highest office, to the great annoyance of the ecclesiasts, he was simultaneously hospitable and inaccessible, a protector who became increasingly rude — ceremonious when he first met with Archbishop Muzzi, apparently friendly and forthright, but in the end he did exactly the opposite of what he had promised. Santiago's ancient aristocracy came to the aid of the apostolic mission. But meanwhile, calumny swelled into an aria of accusation against the foreigners. Muzzi was blamed for applying a law dating from colonial times when he refused to marry a widower to his stepdaughter. The young Mastaï was rumored to have charged an exorbitant sum for performing his ministerial duties in the mansion of a wealthy family. Innuendo, gossip, lies, quarrels and accusations, intrigues and slander — day by day, they became harder for the eminent mandatories to bear. The final blow came when the prophesy of the "young Turks" was fulfilled and freedom of the press was decreed — even though Freire had assured the Roman archbishop that he would never commit such a liberal excess. From that day on, life was impossible for the apostolic delegates. Printed claims were circulated that the inoperative mission had cost the public treasury fifty thousand pesos. The delegates were accused of being spies of the Holy Alliance. And finally, there was a decisive announcement: plans were being made for the secularization of the Chilean clergy, including the nationalization of the Church, which would be exempted from any obedience to Rome . . . Confronted with the reality of the situation — the betrayal of his confidence and good will — Muzzi had no choice but to inform the government that he would be returning to Italy immediately. So, after wasting nine and a half months, the prelate, his young auditor, and Don Salustio traveled to Valparaíso, a tumble-down fishing village surrounded by a circle of mountains, where one heard as much English as Spanish, since the port had several flourishing British businesses to supply the ships — especially the increasingly common North American clippers, trim, sleek ships that amazed everyone with their four-poled masts — stopping there after long, difficult voyages across the South Pacific. Mastaï was already discouraged by the failure of the mission and then suffered the unspeakable agony of losing his stability — a feeling similar to vertigo — when he experienced the telluric effects of two earthquakes, which left him unharmed, but envious of the equanimity of some blind musicians who never stopped playing lively dance tunes during the brief tremors, more concerned about their alms than the geologic furies. The priest was invited to a seaport inn to sample the glorious flavors of foods from Tierra del Fuego — *piure, loco, cochayuyo,* and the giant centerfish — before finally departing on board the *Colombia,* a fast ship with sleek lines and a solid hull, which had already proven herself numerous times, surviving the oceanic furies of the always arduous circumnavigation of the southern tip of America. The air grew colder and two whales appeared as soon as the ship had sailed as far as Valdivia. By November tenth they had reached the island of Chiloé. And on the seventeenth the sailors prepared to brave the terrible passage around Cape Horn.

And there a miracle occurred: the sea was as glassy calm as an Italian lake! There, at the storm-swept end of the continent, a place marked by gigantic black granite monuments under constant attack by a howling southern wind. The captain and sailors of the *Colombia* marveled at this tranquillity—even the saltiest "Cape Horners" could not recall seeing the like of it. A clear, pleasant night descended, in which the happy ship rocked to the regular creaking of the rigging and the gentle swaying of the lanterns. Mastaï leaned against the port gunwale, sensing rather than seeing the southernmost point of the continent, which lay in front of the ship; his thoughts went back over his fitful journey, a peripeteian adventure full of incidents the equal of any in the most popular sea-stories—like the spine-tingling tale of the life raft of the *Medusa:* there had been terrible storms, contrary winds, paralyzing calms, encounters with rare aquatic creatures, even, in the Canary Islands, a raid by buccaneers— who boarded the ship with terrifying screams, slashing the air with their swords, only to suddenly turn respectful and withdraw, contrite, once they realized that the only valuable objects on board the *Héloise* were the monstrance, reliquary, ostensorium, and chalice, which they left in the hands of Archbishop Muzzi, since they were good Catholics, not stinking Protestants. And after that had come the revelation of America, an America more fascinating, varied, and striking than the canon had expected, an America where he discovered so much more than gauchos and *gauderios,* wild Indians, brave bola-twirlers, splendid horsemen, inspired cowboys strumming their guitars and singing of brave deeds and challenges, of love and death and infinity. The biggest surprise was the population: lively, intelligent, and spirited, always productive, if occasionally misguided; Mastaï believed America's population could forge a future the equal of Europe's—especially now that the gap between the old and the new continents had been widened and deepened by the wars of independence. Perhaps the Faith would help to unify the two continents, the young man thought, recalling Chile's many convents and churches, as well as the humble chapels of the pampas, the outpost missions, and the Andean calvaries. But actually—increasing the difference between the two worlds—*here* in America the Faith centered around local cults and a specific constellation of saints who were almost unknown *over there,* in Europe. In fact, when the canon had studied American hagiography in preparation for this trip, he had been astonished at the number of exotics who had become American patrons and saints. Apart from the ineffable mystic Rosa de Lima, whose fame had spread far and wide, American saints were of purely local interest. There was an Andean trinity composed of Rosa and two other (much less well known) figures: Toribio de Lima, born in Majorca, who had served as inquisitor of Philip II and later as archbishop of Peru, in which role he had spent seven years traveling his vast diocese, baptizing an incalculable number of Indians; and Mariana de Peredes, the "Lily of Quito," who emulated Rosa in respect to the mortification of the flesh—during the terrible earthquake of 1645, she had offered her own life to God so that the inhabitants of the city would be spared. After Toribio de Lima came a saint who was little known in the Old World, Francisco Solano; he was in the shipwreck of a slave ship and was responsible for the rescue of the slaves, who had been abandoned by the cowardly crew and left to face the furies of the Atlantic, helpless, without lifeboats or rafts. Next came the famous catechist Luis Beltrán, who had been canonized for the conversion of many Colombian and Panamanian Indians, even though those conversions were

said to be almost worthless, having been made through interpreters because the sainted gentleman was ignorant of the local
languages. The conversions made by the patron of black slaves,
Pedro Claver, were considered more significant; according to his
contemporaries, this energetic adversary of the Holy Office of
Cartagena of the Indies baptized more than three hundred
thousand Africans during his long, exemplary ministry. Next
came some lesser patrons and saints, the objects of merely local
cults: Francisco Colmenario, the Guatemalan preacher, for
example, whose blessed life is little known; and Gregorio
López, former page of King Philip, whose canonization had
gotten nowhere in Rome, even though he was revered in
Zacatecas; or Martín de Porres, barber and surgeon of Lima, the
first mestizo to be beatified; or the Galician holy man, Sebastián
Aparicio—object of a local cult in Pueblo de los Angeles—who
led a secular and mundane life during which he buried two
wives, who was director of the postal service and built roads
between Mexico and Zacatecas, and who had only received the
Faith at seventy. As for Sebastián Montañol, killed by the
Indians of Zacatecas (Zacatecas, like Lima, is definitely a preferred site for the manifestation of transcendental vocations!),
and Alfonso Rodríguez, Juan del Castillo, and Roque González
de Santacruz, the Paraguayan martyrs, their memories were
only preserved in extremely limited areas, in the most remote
regions—there was probably not a single man of the Faith in the
world who remembered them, other than young Mastaï.

No. The ideal, the perfect way to join together the Christian
faithful of the old and new worlds—as an antidote to the
venomous philosophical ideas that had taken too firm a hold in
America—was to find a saint whose acceptance was ecumenical,
a saint whose fame was unlimited, incontrovertible, a saint of
planetary wingspan, a saint so enormous, even larger than the
legendary Colossus of Rhodes, that he could have one foot on
the shores of this continent and the other on the banks of

Europe, with a vision from above the Atlantic that embraced both hemispheres. A Saint Christopher, Christophoros, Porter of Christ, known and admired by everyone, universal in his works and in his prestige. Suddenly, Mastaï had a lightning flash of inspiration: he had thought of the Grand Admiral of Ferdinand and Isabella. With his eyes fixed on the dazzlingly starry sky, he waited for an answer to the question that escaped from his lips. And he thought he could hear the words of Dante:

*I will tell you nothing, so that you
may find the answer within yourself*

But at this point he felt humbled by his awareness of his own insignificance: He would need the authority of a Supreme Pontiff, or, at least, of a prince of the Church, to present a proposal to the Holy Congregation of Rites initiating the canonization of the Grand Admiral — too much time had elapsed since the death of the Discoverer of America, and, to be perfectly frank, his case was somewhat out of the ordinary . . . and he, Mastaï, was only an obscure canon, a mere servant of the court, a defeated participant in a failed apostolic mission. He put his hands over his face that night beneath the immense Cape Horn sky to drive away an idea whose very enormity was beginning to possess him . . . Yes. On that memorable night, he had covered his face with his hands, the same hands that now vacillated between the ink bottle and the quill, the hands of His Holiness Pope Pius IX. Why was he hesitating? He had carried that dream for years, a dream that was on the brink of becoming a reality, that would make the canonization of Christopher Columbus one of the major works of his long papacy. He regarded the document the Primate of Bordeaux had submitted for his attention, slowly rereading a single sentence: *Eminenttissimus quippe Princeps Cardinalis Donnet, Archiepiscopus Burdigalensis, quator ab hine annis exposuit SANCTITATI TUAE venerationem fidelium*

*erga servum Dei Christophorum Columbum, enixe deprecans pro intro-
ductione illius causae exceptionali ordine.**

He turned to the decree attached to the petition and
endorsed it with a firm signature, authorizing the beginning of
the instruction and process. With a sigh of relief and the feeling
of having completed a great task, His Holiness closed the red
binder containing the documents. Quietly opening the door,
Sor Crescencia brought in a lamp whose soft light was diffused
by a green shade, a nightly event announcing the approach of
twilight. He gave the docket to the nun and asked her to see
that it was delivered in the morning, through the customary
channels, to the head of the Holy Congregation of Rites. Then
the pope was alone. Because of his trip to America, he had long
been considered the Vatican's greatest authority on the prob-
lems of America; he had been consulted on all the thorniest
cases and his opinions received with the greatest attention. He
had boasted more than once of being the "first American,
indeed, Chilean, pope."† ("Because I am interested in everything that occurs in those lands across the sea," he said.) But
now he had finally set in motion the intricate mechanism of a
beatification and needed to name a Postulator, a Cardinal
Chairman, a Promoter General of the Faith, a Prothonotary,
and a Chancellor to participate in the process — the first step in
the canonization of Christophoros — only to find himself worrying, once again, about the requirement for a "special procedure": *pro introductione illius causae exceptionali ordine.* Rome
always preferred that the process of beatification begin as soon
as possible after the death of the candidate. When too much

---

*"His Most Eminent Prince Cardinal Donnet, Archibishop of Bordeaux,
made clear, four years ago, the veneration of the faithful for Christopher
Columbus, servant of God, earnestly beseeching that the cause of that
illustrious personage be advanced by special procedure." (Appendix C in the
Postulatum published at the end of *The Revealer of the Globe* by Leon Bloy)

†According to a document published by the Apostolic Nunciature of Chile
(1952).

time had passed, there was always the danger that local devotion had exaggerated what had merely been a pious human life, in which case the Holy Congregation of Rites might grant only a beatification *equipolente* — diminished in force and extent — when what the Supreme Pontiff wanted in the case of Columbus was for the beatification to be universally proclaimed and widely discussed. Because of the passage of time, therefore, the "special procedure" was required. But . . . what about the rest of his case? There could be no doubt of its strength. Thirteen years before, he had requested that Count Roselly of Lorgues, a French Catholic writer, compose a true life of Christopher Columbus, using the most modern documents and information. And that biography — he had read it twenty times — clearly demonstrated that the Discoverer of America was worthy of a place among the major saints. Count Roselly of Lorgues could not have been mistaken. He was a scrupulous, rigorous, dedicated historian, completely trustworthy; and he maintained that the great mariner had lived his entire life with an invisible halo over his head. It was time to make it visible *ad majorem Dei gloriam.* The pope remembered that, just as he himself had, Columbus had belonged to the Third Order of Saint Francis, and that it was a Franciscan who had been his confessor one afternoon in Valladolid . . . Oh, to have been there *that afternoon,* in Valladolid, to have been the obscure friar who had had the immense good fortune to receive the final confession of the Revealer of the Planet! How exciting! On *that afternoon* in Valladolid, how the cosmic images must have flowed, with Columbus's words transforming the poor country estate into a veritable Palace of Marvels! . . . Surely even Ulysses's tales in his allies' courts could not have matched the splendid tales of adventure that emerged *that afternoon* from the mouth of Columbus, who would discover the mysteries of death before nightfall, just as, in life, he had discovered the mysteries of a geographic *beyond,* previously unknown, which men had imagined since the happy age and happy times that Don Quixote spoke of in his discourse to the goatherds, "the happy age and the happy times on which the ancients bestowed the name golden."

II

THE HAND

He has stretched his hand over the sea,

He has shaken the kingdoms.

Isaiah 23:11

hey've gone to get the confessor. But it will take him a long time to get here, because my mule refuses to hurry when the road is bad (mules are fit only for women and clerics anyway); and to get that estimable Franciscan, who has vanquished moral confusion, they have to travel four leagues to the home of one of his relatives who is in need of extreme unction. Since I already have one foot in the grave, I'll use the time to marshal my thoughts, because I'm going to have to talk for a long time to say what I have to say, and I'm more daunted, perhaps, by how much I have experienced than by my illness itself . . . I'll have to tell him everything. Everything, simply everything. I'll have to put my entire self into words and somehow convey even more than the words themselves say—because (and I don't know if a friar can really understand this) *taking action* often entails impulses, constraints, excesses (I concede the word) that, act by act, step by step, are unworthy of the fine words that emerge out of the darkness, finally, and are inscribed next to your name on the tablet of history. The farmer who has shaken the fruit from his neighbor's olive trees is almost innocent as he stands before the Throne of God, as is the whore (pardon my language, but I intend to speak plainly, addressing the highest of the high) who, for want of a better occupation, plies her trade on her back with a sailor in port, while above her hangs a picture of Mary Magdalene, whose holy effigy in Paris graces the banner of the Brotherhood of Rakes, which was recognized as a public treasure—signed and sealed by official decree—by King Louis of France. People like them can make their final confession in a few words. But for those like me who have seen things that were never even imagined before my adventures; for those like me who have sailed into the unknown (and, yes, I admit, I was not the first, I have to admit it; I called it Colchis, thinking that others would understand me better, but Colchis it never was); for those like me who have entered the realm of monsters, torn the veil from mystery, and defied the rages of man and nature — we have much to confess. Things that will be scandalous, unsettling, that will topple truths and expose falsehoods, if only for the friar who will hear me in the privacy of my confession. But at this moment, while I am alive — still — waiting for my final auditor, I am two in one. One, lying down, his hands already folded in prayer, resigned — not so very! — to the death that is coming for him through that door; and the other, looking on from the outside, striving to free himself from the "me" who encloses and imprisons and tries to smother him, crying in Augustine's voice, "My body can no longer bear the weight of my bloody soul." Looking at myself through the eyes of the other who stands by my bed, I see myself like the curiosity I saw on the island of Chios, which a trader at fairs — who was wearing a hat with a zodiac painted on the hatband — showed to me, saying he had found it in the land of Ptolemy: it was a sort of box, in the shape of a man, which contained a second box, similar to the first, which in turn encased the body of a man, who almost looked alive, preserved as he had been by the Egyptians through their arts of embalming. So much vitality was retained in that dry, almost tanned figure, that I thought it might return to life at any moment . . . Stiffening, I still feel the woolen wrapping that envelops my defeated body like that first box; but inside my body, worn down by exhaustion and illness, resides the interior "I," still lucid, keen, of sound mind and memory, witness to marvels, stained with weakness, hedged with caution, repentant today for what I did yesterday, tortured when I regard myself, but calm when I face others, at once frightened and rebellious, a sinner by Divine Will, both actor

and spectator, judge and advocate, my own counsel before the
Tribunal of the Supreme Prosecution where I also occupy the
magistrate's bench and hear the arguments and look at myself,
face to face. And to raise my hands and cry, and indict and reply,
and defend myself against the accusing finger that presses
against my chest, and sentence myself and appeal my sentence,
and reach the highest courts of a judicial system where, finally, I
am alone with myself, with a conscience that accuses me of
much and absolves me of much—alone before the Auditor who
hears our unending explanations; whose face we will never
know; whose very name, for centuries and centuries, could not
be uttered by faithful observers of His Law, people like my
parents and grandparents; and who condescended to let it be
said in His Book that we are made in His image and likeness,
perhaps because He understood that imperfect beings born of
His Infinite Perfection would need an analogy, in His own
image, or their limited understanding would not even begin to
comprehend the universal and ubiquitous image of the One
who propels and regulates the prodigious mechanism of the
planets every day, with infallible punctuality.

. . . But it is not time for me to presume to unveil mysteries that surpass my understanding, it is time for a humility
prompted by the nearness of the end—an end in which the
summoned person, the one placed in the docket, asks himself
whether he will soon be dazzled, consumed, by the fearful
vision of the Likeness Never Seen, or whether he will spend
millennia waiting in the shadows; it is time either to take the
bench of the accused and be sentenced before the bar or to be
lodged in a place of endless waiting by some winged usher, angel
of the notary, with feathered pinions and quills behind his ears,
who is the keeper of the register of souls. But then you remember that such speculations are gravely offensive to the spiritual
rules of your religion, which objects to all vain questions and all
immodest conjectures. You remember, seafarer, the words that

are carved on the stone where every day the faithful tread in the greatest sanctuary of Toledo:

Aquí yace:
Polvo
Ceniza
Nada

Here lies:
Dust
Ash
Nothing

Like *that time,* one day in January, in the clamor of a storm, when a voice — at once loud and clear, near and distant — sounded in his ears: *Oh, foolish one, slow to believe and serve your God, the God of all men. Ever since you were born, He has had great designs for you. Do not fear, but trust in him: all your tribulations are inscribed in marble, and have their purpose.*

So I will speak. I will tell him everything.

f the cardinal sins there is only one that has always been foreign to me, and that is sloth. Because I suffered from lust, I lived a lustful life until I was freed from that sin by greater affairs, and until my soul was completely possessed by a woman with the singular appellation of Madrigal of the High Towers — a name that called to my mind a beautiful song, a regal epiphany, a supreme object of desire — so that even when I first looked upon those mountains that no Christian had ever seen before, their shape immediately reminded me of those other soft, heaving mounds etched in the most secret recesses of my memory . . . Ever since my father, without giving up his wool business, opened a cheese and wine store in Savona — with a back room where the customers could carry their glasses to the spigot and bang them together on a thick walnut table — I liked to listen to the stories of the seafaring men, emptying bottle after bottle of red wine, which they secretly shared with me — wine I've enjoyed so much ever since that many people later in my life were amazed that I always carried a huge quantity of wine casks on my seafaring ventures and that, when I came to think of agricultural endeavors, I always reserved the best lands that Divine Providence had granted me for the sowing and cultivating of wine. Noah, who was the ancestor of all navigators, was the first to set a bad example; and since wine heats the blood and incites lewd appetites, there was no brothel in the Mediterranean that didn't know my youthful passion when I took to the sea, to my father's disgust . . . I knew the women of Sicily, Chios, Cyprus, Lesbos, and other islands where the population was a mixture of half-converted Moors, new Christians who still refuse to eat pork, Syrians who make the sign of the cross in front of any church without knowing what denomination it is, and Greeks who are ready to sell their sisters at any hour, while the church bells chime, and don't mind trafficking in sodomy and buggery if that's what's wanted. I penetrated them all: women who played the ambuca and timbrel to put me in the mood; "Genoans" dressed like Jewesses, who gave me a complicitous wink to whet my desire; women with alcoholic eyes who made the butterflies tattooed on their bellies flutter when they danced; others — almost always Moors — who held the money I gave them in their mouths to defend their tongues against other intruding tongues; and women who swore and blasphemed, who still looked young from behind, at least when some appreciable generosity led them to grant — rare favor! — what they never granted anyone; and Alexandrians, their faces caked with powder, rouged and painted, like figureheads on a ship — like the dead portrayed on the outer lids of the sarcophagi that are still used in their country; and those from all over who howl that they'll pass out, that you're killing them, that they're already dead, that there's no one like you, and they finish you off in three bumps and three grinds, while they overcome your indifference by covering their loins with a succession of tales intended to cause a pleasure so vocalized that you would pay just to listen . . . All those I knew, and many more in rough Sardinia and Marseilles, city of extravagant vice, even though it wasn't until years later that, sailing the African coast, I knew the dark-skinned women — always darker — until I reached the darkest ones of Guinea, of the Gold Coast, with their knife-inscribed cheeks, adorned with pearls threaded through their eight braids, woolly hair sticking out, and abundant buttocks, whom the Portuguese and Galicians so rightly favored — and I say "rightly," because I seem to remember that if King Solomon was wise for his Solomonic judgments and learned governing, he was also wise in allying himself with the woman — *nigra sum* . . . — whose breasts were like clusters of grapes, of the black, swollen grapes ripened at the foot of the mountains, in sea breezes, and made into a heavy, fragrant wine that, when it is drunk, leaves its savorous imprint on the lips . . . But man does not live by flesh alone, and in my voyages I had the good fortune to learn the arts of navigation—although, to tell the truth, I put more faith in my ability to gauge the smell of the winds, decipher the language of the clouds, and interpret the changing colors of the water than in using calculations and instruments as my guide. I was fascinated by the flight of both sea and land birds, because they can be better informed than man in judging the directions that are most favorable. I understood the wisdom of the Hyperboreans who—I've been told—carried two crows on their ships to be set free when they lost their orientation in some unfavorable navigation, because they knew that if the birds didn't return to the ship, they needed only to set sail in the direction the birds had flown to find land in a few miles. This wisdom of the birds led me to study the peculiarities and habits of some of the animals of the universe that astonish us, with our limited understanding, by the ways they live and join and procreate. Thus, I knew that the rhinoceros—*in nare cornus*—in its rampages can be soothed only by a maiden who exposes her chest as he approaches, and "in that manner" (Saint Isadoro of Seville tells us) "the animal will grow calm and rest his head on the young woman's breasts." I had not seen this marvel of nature, but I knew that the basilisk, queen of the serpents, kills creatures that resemble it on sight, so that no bird can escape it. I knew of the saurian, a small lizard that crawls into a hole in a wall that faces east when it is old and blind, and then turns to the sun as it rises, and takes strength from it, and recovers its sight. I was also interested in the salamander, which, as everybody knows, lives in the middle of flames without being harmed or consumed by them; a fish called the stargazer, because it has an eye in its head that looks up at the sky; and the sucking-fish, schools of which can halt a ship so completely that it seems rooted to the ocean floor; and, like all creatures of the sea, I was particularly interested in the swallow that nests on the ocean in winter and raises its young there on the water—and Saint Isadoro also tells us that when the young birds hatch, the elements become calm and the winds die down for seven days, as nature pays tribute to that bird and its young. Each day I found more pleasure in studying the world and its wonders—and from so much study I became convinced that I had opened secret doors to reveal marvels and mysteries unsuspected by most mortals. I wanted to know it all. I envied King Solomon—"wiser than Heman, Kalkol, and Darda"—who was able to speak of all the trees, from the cedar that is from Lebanon to the hyssop that roots in walls, and who also knew the customs of all the four-legged animals, the birds, the reptiles, and the fish of the universe. And why shouldn't he know everything? Wasn't he informed about everything by his messengers, ambassadors, tradesmen, and seamen? From Ophir and Tarsus they brought him shipments of gold. In Egypt they bought his chariots, and in Cilicia they procured his horses; and his stables in turn provided chargers for the kings of the Hittites and the kings of Aram. Moreover, he was informed about an infinite variety of things—virtues of plants, relationships of beasts, and lewd and lascivious acts, and the contumelies, ignominies, and sodomies of different peoples—by his women, Moabite, Ammonite, Edomite, Sondian, not to mention the Egyptians—and very fortunate was he, that wise, depraved man, that in his marvelous palace he could choose, according to each day's whim, from seven hundred principal wives and three hundred concubines, not counting guests, travelers, unexpected visitors, the woman from Sheba, for example, who paid him to have her. (Secret dream of all true men!) And yet the world known by King Solomon was so vast and diverse that I couldn't help concluding that his fleet of ships really went only to places that were known. They had never gone beyond, all they could bring back were tales of those monsters mentioned by the travelers and sailors who had crossed the thresholds of territories that even now are virtually unknown. According to witnesses of unquestioned authority, to this very day there are races of people in the Far East who have faces that are entirely flat, without any noses; and there are others whose lower lips are so prominent that they use them to cover their faces when they want to sleep or be in the shade; still others have such small mouths they have to ingest their food through oat straws; and there are some who have no tongues and communicate only by signs and gestures. In Scythia there are people known as Panotians, who have such large ears that they can wrap themselves in them, as in a cape, to keep themselves warm. In Ethiopia live the Sciopodes, who are remarkable for their legs and their swiftness in running; in winter they lie on the ground and shelter themselves with their feet, which are so long and broad they can use them as sunshades. In such countries, there are men who live only on perfumes, others who have six hands, and most marvelous of all, women who give birth to fully grown people—people who are rejuvenated and become children in their old age. And, without traveling so far, remember the story of Saint Jerome, that supreme doctor, who tells of discovering a faun or a goat-man who was exhibited in Alexandria and became an excellent Christian, against the expectations of everyone accustomed to consign such beings to the legends of paganism . . . What's more, though many men may brag about knowing Libya, they're probably quite unaware of the existence of the dreadful men born there without heads, with their eyes and mouths where we have nipples and navels. And it seems that in Libya there are also *antipodes,* who have the soles of their feet reversed and eight toes on each foot. But reports are divided about the *antipodes,* and some travelers say that they include an appalling variety of dog-headed men, cyclops, troglodytes, ant-people, and headless men, not to mention men with two faces, like the god Janus of the ancients . . . But I don't really think that is how the *antipodes* look. I am convinced—although it is entirely a personal opinion—that the *antipodes* are completely different: they are simply the creatures mentioned by Saint Augustine, even though the Bishop of Hippo denied their existence and mentioned them only because of all the talk about them. If bats can sleep hanging by their feet, if many insects can move quite easily across the ceiling of the whore's room where I am presently pursuing these thoughts — while the woman is out getting wine at a nearby tavern — then surely there can exist human beings capable of going without heads or with their heads underneath, whatever the venerable author of the *Enchiridion* may say. There are acrobats who spend half their lives walking on their hands without the sanguinary humors flowing into their temples, and there are people in the Indies who claim to be saints and rest on their elbows for months with their legs in the air, holding their bodies perfectly still. There is a portent to be found in the tales of men like Jonah, who spent three days and three nights in the belly of a whale, with his forehead plastered with seaweed, breathing as if he were in his natural environment. We deny many things because our limited understanding makes us think them impossible. But as I continued reading and educating myself, I kept on finding that things I had thought were impossible were in fact real. To believe them one has only to read the reports and chronicles of the brave traders, the great navigators — especially the great navigators like Pitheas, the mariner from Marseilles who was trained in Phoenician rowing techniques and who pointed his vessel northward, ever northward, in an insatiable desire for discovery, until he reached a place where the sea congealed like the ice on mountain peaks. More and more I realized that I had still not read enough. I would have to read more books. Especially books that described voyages. I had heard of a tragedy written by Seneca about Jason leading a band of argonauts west of the Pontus Euxinus, where they discovered the golden fleece of Colchis. I would have to become familiar with Seneca's tragedy, which, according to the ancients, contained so many valuable lessons.

The hoarse, echoing, drawn-out notes of the trumpets descend cheerlessly from the top of the smaller mast of the slow-moving ship, lost in billows of fog so thick that from the sterncastle you can't make out the prow. The sea, extending unbroken in all directions, looks like a lake of lead, with calm ripples describing diminutive crests that flatten out without ever breaking into whitecaps. The watch shout out his call, but no one answers. Again the questioning cry is raised and then lost in the lulling silence of the cloud that close in upon me, twenty varas away, and I am left alone — alone with a sailor's phantoms — in tense anticipation. Because of the emotion raised by the watch's cry, because of my anxiety to see, I press myself against the gunwales as soon as the sextant's bell sounds. And though I have sailed all over the world, today I find myself on an unknown course on a voyage that retains the flavor of heroism — and I can't say that about my one-day runs in the Mediterranean. I am impatient to catch a glimpse of this strange land — they say that it is strange indeed! — which marks the end of the earth. Since leaving Bristol we have had favorable winds and favorable seas, and it seems there will be no repetition of my ordeal off Cape San Vicente where, by the divine will of the Lord, I was rescued, clinging to an oar, after the horrible wreck of a flaming storeship. In Galloway we picked up Master Jacob, foremost authority on these aquamarine routes, who worked for Spinola and Di Negro, guiding their ships full of lumber and wine. It seems that since there are neither trees nor grapevines on the island we are approaching, wood and wine are the things its inhabitants value most: lumber for building their houses; wine for raising their

45

spirits during the interminable winter when the very ocean congeals around them, its waves frozen into ice—the drifting mountains that Pitheas of Marseilles had reported seeing—shutting them off from the world. At least that's what I was told, but Master Jacob, who knows these regions well, maintains that the sea did not freeze at all this year—nor did it in several other years—because certain currents from the west temper the rigors of the season . . . This Master Jacob is a pleasant, jovial companion, who now resides in remote Galloway, where he lives with a beautiful Scottish woman, young, freckled, and large-breasted, who is not too concerned with questions of the purity of bloodlines that so preoccupy the rulers of Spain these days. It has long been rumored that soon—next month, one of these days, no one knows when—the tribunals of the Inquisition will begin to investigate and record the past, the progenitors, the origins of the new Christians. It will no longer suffice to forswear apostasy, but each convert will be called to account, retroactively, for anything he has been seen doing that raises the suspicion of fraud, dissimulation, indifference, or falsehood, to the delight of any debtor, any coveter of a neighbor's goods, any cunning enemy—of any seamstress of hymens or caster of the evil eye, interested in turning attention from his own business of charms and love potions. But there is more: a saying that started no one knows where, a joke that has been passed from mouth to mouth, foretelling unhappy times ahead. The saying—as I've heard it—goes *Hey, Jews, better pack your bags. . .* It may be meant as a joke, but the joke could get rough and turn into the reality of a new exodus—which my Lord certainly cannot want, since so many riches proceed from the Jews, and the Santángels, those great financiers, have filled the royal tills with a "loan" of thousands and thousands of coins stamped with the die of their circumcisions. Master Jacob believes that a prudent man counts for two, that it's time to begin the diaspora, and so, with the aid of the firm of Spinola and Di Negro, he has decided to put down stakes in Galloway, where he runs their supply store by the side of his buxom, freckled, big-breasted girl, who makes his life sweet, even if she sometimes smells too strong, like a lot of redheads. Moreover, he possesses a skill that has made him indispensable: his prodigious ability to learn a language in a few days. He speaks Portuguese as easily as Provençal; the language of Genoa or Picardy as fluently as the English of London, the jargon of Britain; he is even conversant with the abrupt language, bristling with consonants, stutters, and snores — "the language of sneezing inward" he calls it — that is employed in the gloomy island toward which we are sailing — an island enveloped in fog, though the dark outlines of its shape begin to appear on the horizon now, a little after the last canonical hour. We have reached the end of the earth! . . .

I don't know why Master Jacob looks at me askance every time I talk about the "end of the earth." And now that we are on land, in a sturdy pine house, passing the resined wineskin back and forth, Master Jacob, his voice a little loud from drink, makes fun of the notion that this is the end of the known world. He says that even the bald-headed infants in soggy diapers who crawl in the streets of this port whose name they can't even say, even they would laugh at me if I told them that this ground we're standing on is the limit or end of anything. And, recounting marvel after marvel, he tells me that these men of the north (*Normans,* they are therefore called, it seems), when we had barely emerged from the womb to make our first tentative search for new sea routes, had already traveled to the land of the *Russes* in the east, and having turned their light and well-armed boats to the rivers of the south, had already reached the kingdoms of Gog and Magog and the sultanates of Arabia, where they obtained coins that they are proud to display, such trophies obtained in some Chersonese peninsula . . . And to show he wasn't lying, Master Jacob showed me some denarii and dirhams from the districts where the remote ancestors of these tribes had traveled, which he kept like talismans in his mariner's handkerchief—even though his religion, as I know so well, prohibits the practice of such superstitions. The Master takes the wineskin, squirts a large draft of wine down his gullet, swallows, and turns his eyes to the west. He tells me how, long ago, as much as several centuries ago, a redheaded man from these parts, condemned to exile for a murder he had committed, had undertaken a voyage that led him far from the usual routes, to an enormous country he called "Green Land," because of the green trees he found there. "Impossible!" I tell Master Jacob, citing the greatest cartographers of the age, all of whom are ignorant of that Green Land, which has never been mentioned by our greatest sailors. Master Jacob gives me a shrewd look and tells me that more than two hundred years ago there were already a hundred ninety farms in Green Land, two convents of nuns, and even a dozen churches—one of them almost as large as the grandest the Normans had built in their lands. And that was not all. Lost in the fog, sailing phantasmal ships through hyperborean nights without dawn, cutting through the clouds by candlelight, those men dressed in hides had traveled even farther to the west, and then still farther, discovering islands, unknown lands, which had been mentioned in a treatise entitled *Inventio fortunata,* which I didn't know, but which Master Jacob seems to have studied closely. But there was even more. Sailing ever westward, farther and farther westward, a son of the redheaded mariner, called "Leif the Lucky," reached an immense land that he named "Wood Land." In that land salmon abounded, fruits and berries were plentiful, the trees were enormous, and—a marvel at that latitude—the vegetation did not die back in winter. Moreover, the coast was not craggy and forbidding, nor was it plagued with underwater caves where the ocean roared and terrible dragons dwelled . . . Leif the Lucky traveled inland in that unknown paradise until a German sailor named Tyrkir disappeared from his party. Several days passed, and just when his companions had concluded they would never see him again, that he had been devoured by some unknown, ferocious monster, Tyrkir reappeared, as drunk as a lord, announcing that he had discovered enormous wild vines whose grapes had started to ferment and had produced a wine that, well, just look at me, no one here can challenge me, I'll just sleep it off, this is Valhalla, and I'm not going to leave, don't anyone try to stop me, because if they do I'll lop their heads off the way Beowulf decapitated that dragon with the poison fangs, I'm the king here, and anyone who says different . . . And then he fell flat on the ground and vomited and wailed that all Normans are sons of bitches . . . But from that day on the Normans knew that past Green Land lay "Vinland" . . . "And if you think I'm lying," says Master Jacob, "consult the writings of Adam of Bremen and Oderico Vital." But I don't know where to find those books, which are probably written in a language I don't understand. What I want is for him to tell me, to relate the stories they are still telling here — on this island where jets of boiling water spew out of holes in black rocks — singing and playing the harp, those preservers of memories of ancient sagas called *skalds*. And my dark friend tells me that when the men here learned of the existence of Vinland, they soon made another voyage there, a hundred and sixty men, under the command of a certain Thorvald, another son of the redheaded outcast, and his brother-in-law Thorstein, who was married to a woman who wore a sword in her belt and a knife between her breasts, and who was named Freydis. And again they found the abundant salmon, the acidic wine with its pleasing intoxication, the vegetation that never died back, the young larches, and they even discovered, farther inland, vast fields of wild wheat. And everything seemed pleasing and delightful, when suddenly there appeared boats that seemed to be made from the hides of water creatures, which were paddled by small men with coppery skin, prominent cheekbones, rather elongated eyes, with air like the manes of horses, whom the large, coarse, fair-skinned men considered quite ugly and malformed. At first they entered into trade with them and things went well. They made magnificent exchanges that worked to their advantage. They obtained valuable skins in return for whatever seemed new to those men with whom they communicated by signs: cheap brooches, amber beads, glass necklaces, and, especially, red cloth — because it seemed that they were particularly attracted by the color red, which was highly prized by the Normans as well. And everything was fine until the day a bull, which had been brought along in one of the ships, escaped from his pen and began to roam the coast. No one knew what happened to the little men: they began a frantic flight, as if something had driven them mad, perhaps some sign of evil according to their pagan religion; but the little men came back later, swarming, climbing, fast-moving hordes of them, hurling stones, showers of pebbles, avalanches of gravel, upon the fair-skinned giants whose axes and swords proved useless in this kind of warfare. It was no use for the woman Freydis to expose her breasts to shame those men without balls who were fleeing for the ship. And, taking the sword of a fallen warrior, she threw herself upon the stone-flinging hordes, who were terrified by the cries of the dreadful woman and soon fled in turn . . . But that night, gathered together in council, the *Vikings* — as they were sometimes called — agreed to return home to outfit a new expedition with more men, better armed. That project, however, kindled little enthusiasm among people who dealt with the known world year after year, sending their ships to Paris, Sicily, and Constantinople. Nobody in those days wanted to risk the dangers of an inauspicious foothold in a land where their enemies — men, beasts — are not as frightening — since they are a danger that is known — as the mysteries of the mountains that had barely been glimpsed, rising abruptly out of the plains; of caves that might hold monsters; of the endless empty spaces; of brushlands where they heard wails, cries, and laments in the night, proving that there were spirits in the land—a land so vast, extending so far to the south, that it would take thousands and thousands of men and women to explore and populate it. So they did not return to the vast western land, and the image of Vinland has faded into the distance, like a mirage, lingering only as a marvelous memory in the legends of the *skalds,* so that its real existence is consigned to the great book by Adam of Bremen, historian to the Archbishop of Hamburg, who was charged with carrying the cross of Christ to the hyperborean lands, either known or not yet discovered, where the word of the Gospels had never been heard. And it was good that the Word be heard in those lands, since there are men living there, many men, who are ignorant of Him who died for their sins—and there are other men like them, or so they say, who ride in sleds pulled by dogs to travel to the land of eternal night . . . I asked Master Jacob for the name of those beings—surely the dupes of treacherous idolatries—who had the courage to throw the fair-skinned giants of the north out of their kingdom. "I don't know what they call themselves," the mariner replied. "In the language of the discoverers they are called *skraelings,* which means—how would we say it?—something like deformed, humpbacked, bandy-legged people. Yes. That's it: bandy-legged. Because of course the Normans are tall and handsome. And those people, short, squat, flat-faced, seemed deformed to them. *Skraelings.* That is: bandy-legged." "I'd say *manikins.*" "That's it, that's it," exclaimed Master Jacob, "*manikins.* That's the very word!"

It is late when I return to my room in the shop of Spinola and Di Negro, which contains so much wood piled in heaps, and so many casks brought here to hold a drink they call *biorr,* that it smells, in this remote land, of Spanish resin. But I cannot sleep. I think of those seafarers wandering through fogs and empty spaces, their fantastic ships crowned with heads of dragons, coming upon green mountains sketched over uncertain horizons, running against floating logs, smelling breezes bearing new scents, fishing from the water leaves of unknown form, wandering mandrake roots created in unknown bays; I see those men obscured in the mist, barely discernible, testing the flavor of the currents, judging the saltiness of the foam, reading the language of the waves, watching the flight of rare birds, the passage of a school of fish amid a drift of seaweed. Everything I learned from my voyages, all my *imago mundi,* all my *speculum mundi,* came back to me . . . So then, sailing to the west, one finds an immense *terra firma,* populated by manikins, extending seemingly endlessly to the south? And I say that it is therefore possible that it stretches to the torrid zones, perhaps to the latitude of Malagueta, since those Normans found salmon and grapevines. And salmon—except in the Pyrenees, where they are a great rarity, the way everything is a rarity in that land—end where grapes begin. And the grape goes as far as Andalusia, to the Greek islands that I know well, to the Madeiras, and it seems that it even reaches to the land of the Moors, although they do not make wine from it because that is prohibited by the Koran. But, according to what I have learned, where the grape ends, dates begin. And perhaps dates are also found in that world, to the south, south of the grape . . . In that case . . . I rearrange, rotate, turn upside down, sketch and redraw all the known maps. Better to forget the maps, since they quickly make me irritated, annoyed by their arrogant pretension that they contain everything. It would be better to turn to the poets who sometimes made accurate prophesies in the best metered verse. I open the book of Seneca's *Tragedies* that I brought with me on my voyage. I linger over the tragedy of *Medea,* which pleases me with its accounts of the Pontus and Scythia, of journeys, of suns and stars, of the constellations of Capricorn and even of the Bears that had bathed in forbidden waters, and I pause at the final strophe of the sublime chorus that sings of the adventures of Jason:

. . . Venient annis
saecula seris quibus Oceanus
uincula rerum laxet et ingens
pateat tellus Tethysque nouos
detegat orbes nec sit terris
ultima Thule . . .

I take a quill and translate as best I can, into Spanish, which still comes slowly to me, those verses that I would recite so often in the coming years: *There will come in the late years of the world certain times in which the Ocean will wash over the land and a great land will be opened and a new mariner resembling Jason, named Typhis, will discover a new world, and then the island Thule will no longer be the farthest point on earth.* That night the strings of the harp and the *skalds'* stories of adventure vibrated in my mind, the way that the strings of the great harp that was the ship of the argonauts resonated in the wind.

seem to have been bewitched by the sound of Master Jacob's voice. Again and again I go over the smallest details of the marvelous discovery made by those men of the north, whose story has reached us through their *sagas* — as they call their romances, which, like those of Infantes de Lara or *The Romance of the Cid*, preserve great, unfailing truths behind the pleasing artifice of the studied language and florid rhetoric added by their clerical scribes. And I ponder, especially, the question of distances. The voyage out must have seemed long to the sailors — the way unknown routes always seem to us, when we don't know how long we're going to be traveling — but, really, it must not be far from the Land of Ice (*Ice-landia,* as they call it in their language, which is the Thile or Thule of the ancients), to that land of salmon and grapes, from which the explorers were driven — and I am amazed that they showed so little courage — by a handful of manikins with neither swords nor spears. After all, the romances of this island also relate how Leif the Lucky went from Nidaros to Vinland without stopping; and again, how he sailed a single, straight course from Vinland to Ice-landia on his return. And their ships are certainly superbly built, light, tall, of good length, very seaworthy. But it's also true that they are rather narrow, not as broad-waisted as they ought to be. If they had to make a long voyage, they would soon run short of necessary provisions. So Vinland must be near, quite near, and the miraculous thing is that no one else has sailed there, following the men of the north. And if what I have learned is not generally known, it may be for this reason: of the few mariners from Genoa, Lisbon, or Seville who came to Ice-land, which they thought was the end of the

54

world, none knew the language of sneezes — with all its grunting and rasping — as well as Master Jacob does, and since (to put it plainly) Master Jacob is not one to drink in port with the common seamen, crude and ill-mannered, who man our ships, none of them had the good fortune to hear his tales, except for me, because, to tell the truth, our brief but cordial friendship results from a brotherhood which is — we might say — below the belt . . . The fact is that now the years rushed confusedly past my eyes. I was certain that there was a great, populous, and rich land to the west; I believed that by sailing west I would be sure to reach it. But even though I was convinced, as a result of the stories I had heard in the Land of Ice, that sailing west would be safe, if I said as much, the merit of my enterprise would be diminished. Worse yet: a sovereign could easily choose some familiar, favored, confident, brilliant captain to command the ships in my place and snatch away the glory I would achieve as Discoverer, which I hold higher than any other honor. My ambition forced me to keep my knowledge secret. So I could not reveal the truth. And since I had to keep it quiet, I got caught in such a web of fabulous stories that only in my full confession can I finally disentangle them and reveal to the astonished Franciscan who hears it that — with my mind always inflamed with the same thoughts; pursued night and day by the same idea; unable to open a book without trying to find, in the background, a verse, a portent of my mission; seeking presages, applying oneiromancy to the interpretation of my dreams, which led me to consult the texts of the Pseudo-Joseph and the Alphabetic Keys of the Pseudo-Daniel, and, therefore, the tract of Artemidorus of Ephesus; living such a feverish, disturbed life, designing more or less fantastic plans — that I became a tremendous and unabashed fake: that is the word, I must admit; yes, I must admit, looking at myself in my final hours, that others, less fraudulent, much less fraudulent than I, were made to blush for their pallid fictions on the great stage of the Holy Office.

Because they seem insignificant, the impostures of those who trick a lovesick youth by selling him love potions or advance dishonorable designs by using popular witchcraft, prescribing unguents of bear, or snake, or hedgehog, cemetery dust, or concoctions of tree bark, or bladders, or golden beaks and deep-colored leaves, or charms from Clivicula de Salomon: they seem insignificant, the intrigues of pimps and madams, those who invoke the Prince of Darkness, who is too busy with bigger jobs to bother with such trifles—I repeat, they all seem quite insignificant compared to the deceptions and intrigues I practiced for years and years, trying to gain the favor of the princes of the earth, hiding the real truth behind feigned truths, citing authority for my claims with allusions expertly selected from the Writings, never revealing in my conclusions Seneca's prophetic lines:

> . . . *Venient annis*
> *saecula seris quibus Oceanus*
> *uincula rerum laxet. . . .*

And so I went from court to court. I didn't care who would sponsor my journey. I needed ships to sail, and I would take them wherever I could get them. Solid ships, broad-waisted, with experienced pilots and men with hair on their chests—it didn't matter to me if they came from the galleys. I didn't need chaplains. I just wanted to get *over there*—that would be an achievement in itself!—I didn't want to be tied down with doctrinal or theological obligations, since I didn't know if those manikins subscribed to some barbarous religion that would be difficult to eradicate, requiring the offices of learned men with experience in preaching to the gentiles and converting idolaters. The first thing was to cross the ocean: the Gospels could follow afterward—we would go alone. As for the glory to be achieved by my enterprise, whichever king received the worldly honor, my glory would be the same, and I would reap the full harvest of personal honors and benefits achieved. So I contrived a work-shop of marvels, like those the goliards make in Italian fairs. I launched into my theatrics before dukes and monarchs, financiers and friars, rich men, clerics and bankers, the great men from here and there; I erected a curtain of words, from behind which appeared, in a dazzling procession, the grand illusions of Gold, Diamonds, Pearls, and, especially, Spices. Doña Cinnamon, Doña Nutmeg, Doña Pepper, and Doña Cardamom entered on the arm of Don Ginger and Don Clove, to the beat of a tune whose musical harmonies resonated with the color of saffron and the smell of malabar and the names of Cipango, Cathay, the Golden Colchis, and all the Indies—which, as everyone knows, are many—the numerous, proliferous, epicene, and beautiful Indies, indistinct but moving toward us, wanting to reach out to us, to annex themselves to our laws, close—closer than we thought, though they still seemed distant—the Indies that we now can reach straightaway, sailing to the left-hand side of the maps, scorning the ill-fated route of the right hand, which was plagued in those days by Moslem pirates and buccaneers sailing Chinese junks, while on the land route they imposed outrageous tolls, transit fees, impositions of weights and measures, in the territories ruled by the Great Turk . . . Left hand. Right hand. Open them, show them, move them with the dexterity of a juggler, with the delicacy of spun gold, or instead, be dramatic and raise them in prophesy, quoting Isaiah, invoking the Psalms, lighting Roman candles, exposing the forearm as the sleeve falls back, suggesting the invisible, signaling the unknown, scattering riches, holding up treasures as numerous as the imaginary pearls that still appeared to slip through my fingers, falling to the ground and bouncing in an oriental play of light from the amaranth of the rugs. The nobles and counselors applauded, praised my original notions, momentarily considered my promises of visionary goldsmithery, of alchemy without retorts, but in the end they showed me the door—the doors—with neither ships nor expectations . . . And so I went on for years and years, shouldering my bag of tricks, without the word of Seneca becoming flesh in the flesh of the one who lies here now, sweaty and ailing, defeated in body, waiting for the Franciscan confessor, to tell him everything, everything . . .

nd I will tell him how, while I waited for the chance to fulfill my desire, to begin the most fabulous undertaking ever known — and the waiting was the worst of the business for me, in the final analysis — I was in Lisbon, and I believed, like the poet, that "the world strives for two things": first "to be fed," and second "to find a good woman." I saw Felipa and courted her like the worldly gentleman that I am. Although she was young-looking and had a lovely body, she was a widow with few resources and a daughter to support. But since I knew she was from a good family, that did not matter too much to me, and I led her to the altar of the church where we had met one day as she arose from her devotions, since she was more than just a good-looking woman — she was, after all, related by marriage to the Braganzas and that would open the door (actually, more than one thing would open up for me in this marriage) through which I would enter the Portuguese court, where I could display my bag of tricks. But then began the hard years of waiting: at first on the island of Puerto Santo, where I went to live with my Felipa, and even her satisfying presence — and again I cite the poet — which was "in love, ardent; in bed, comforting, playful, and laughing," was not enough to keep me from feeling restless when I saw a growing number of signs of what was hidden beyond the horizon that I gazed upon every day. On the beaches of that island enormous trunks of trees unknown in the terra firma of Europe wash ashore, and strangely shaped plants with three-lobed leaves, which seem to have fallen from a star. Someone told me about an extraordinary piece of wood carried in by the waves, which seemed to have been carved by people who were ignorant of our iron tools and used fire to work it as we would use a saw and a plane; and people also told me about a great event, the discovery several years before of the bodies of two men "with very broad faces" and unusual physiques — this last story seemed unlikely to me, though, because it was hard to believe that those bodies could have traveled so far without being reduced to bones by the many voracious fish in the ocean, where, if the known ones are unimaginably numerous, the unknown ones are countless and monstrous — there are those with the heads of unicorns, those with mouths spouting torrents of water — every bit as monstrous as that sea serpent, the daughter of Leviathan and Onoco, who traveled by sea to the Asian Galatia on the banks of the Rhone, wrapping herself around whatever ship she saw with such fury that she reduced the ship's timbers to splinters and sank its crew and cargo . . . I won't go into detail about the petty business and voyages I undertook in the days after the little son I named Diego was born. But when I was left a widower — free of a union that had to some degree tempered my impatience — the fire of my ambition began to burn once again and I resolved to seek aid wherever I could find it — and it was a good time for me to act, since Portuguese sailors were growing bolder and bolder in their explorations and less and less fearful about looking to the east and the south, so that soon they would surely begin to look to the west, which was, legitimately, my territory, ever since Master Jacob had first inspired my spirit of adventure. Whenever I received any news of Portuguese voyages I was filled with anxiety. Every day, every night I shook with the fear that they would steal the sea — my sea — the way that the misers in Latin satires tremble before imagined thieves. This ocean that I look out on from the pine-covered shores of Puerto Santo belonged to me, and with each passing week the danger grew that it would be taken from me. And I was seized again by the thoughts and desires that had been passionately aroused in me on board the ships of Centurione and Di Negro — recently merged — whose sugar business I handled, making regular short runs from Madeira to the Gold Coast, from Flores to Genoa, and back to the Azores and back to Genoa, buying, selling, carrying, conducting business, when I knew I was capable of greater things, of giving the world a new image of what was, in reality, the World. *Imago mundi! Speculum mundi!* Only I, an obscure sailor, who grew up between the cheeses and wines in a tavern, knew the true meaning of those words. But now it was time for action. Maps, texts, there was nothing left for me to learn. And since I needed the help of a king to underwrite my enterprise, I resolved to look long and hard, far and wide, for that help. It didn't really matter to me, when all was said and done, which nation I would help to gain infinite glory and limitless riches. I wasn't Portuguese or Spanish or English or French. I was Genoan, and Genoans are citizens of the world. I had to visit every court I could, without worrying too much about who would benefit from my success, whether the crown that sponsored me was the enemy of this, that, or the other. So I dusted off my bag of tricks and took it on a new tour of the continent. First I exhibited it in Portugal, where I encountered a king who was stuffed full of cosmographies, teleologies, maritime geographies, and so trusting of his navigators that they were starting to swell up as if they were pregnant, and who, when I finished my stories referred me to the authority of several doctors, geographers, canons, and to the idiotic bishop of Ceuta—not that Ceuta was Antioquía!—and to masters Rodríguez and Joseph, who were cruder and more ignorant than the whorish mothers who bore them, all of whom reached the conclusion that my arguments were simply variations and new versions, like in the art of bel canto, of themes already sung by Marco Polo—the great Venetian whose book I had read with admiration but in whose footsteps I had no desire to follow since what I most wanted to do was to arrive, by sailing with the sun, at those countries that he had traveled to by sailing against the sun. If his travels had described a semicircle around the Earth, it was up to me to draw the second half. But I knew — and knew well — that the missing section to complete the circumference corresponded to the Nation of the Manikins. So, disenchanted with Portugal, I packed my bag of tricks and went to exhibit it in Córdoba, where Their Catholic Majesties regarded it with suspicion. I found the Aragonese king to be silly, weak, and without character, dominated by his condescending wife who, during the audience I had been granted, barely paid attention to my words, as if her mind were on other matters. And I left there with the meager promise that their counselors — it was the same story all over again! — would think about my proposal, because, just then, the many pressing concerns of government, and the high costs of the war, and blah blah blah: empty evasions of a sovereign who was full of herself, who wanted to show off how well read she was, who said she felt "so foolish," poor thing, "when she had to match wits with the theologians of Toledo" — the false humility of someone who pretends to apologize for her limited knowledge, when in fact she thinks she knows it all. I was furious when I left the interview, and it wasn't simply anger — I had never liked doing business with women, except in bed, and it was clear that at this court it was the woman who was in charge and gave the orders . . . But since you can't live without women — though for other reasons — I began living with a handsome Biscayan woman, who gave me another son. We never talked about marriage, and I didn't want to, because this time I wasn't sleeping with someone who was related to the Braganzas or the Medinacelis, and I must admit, besides, that as soon as I got astride her I could tell she had been down this road as often as I had. Which didn't stop me, of course, from following where other men had been before, on that pearl-white filly, without bridle or stirrups, while my brother Bartholomew went to show off my bag of tricks in England, at the throne of the first Tudor king. But he quickly realized that he would never get a warm reception there, because those dirty Englishmen didn't know a thing about seafaring—incapable as they had proven to be of getting even a bundle of cinnamon sticks or a small bag of pepper except from a spice shop. Then he thought he would try the king of France, who was richer than his mother now that he had made a good marriage and become the Duke of Brittany. But for the Bretons of Duchess Anne, the whale and the herring, sperm and brine, were surer bets than the gold of the Indies, and there too he failed to win a favorable audience. Yet despite the failures and setbacks I continued to press my case. When I realized that you can obtain a fair hearing only if you carry some weight, intimidate the ushers, look impatient in the waiting rooms, and string titles and honors after your name, I made up an imaginary past designed to take the place of the Savona tavern—honor thy father and thy mother!—with its dealer in wool and cheese behind his barrels and taps joining in daily riots with penniless drunkards. I quickly pulled out of my sleeve an uncle who was an admiral; and I made myself a graduate of the University of Pavía in whose cloisters I had never set foot in my whole damned life; I made myself the friend—without ever having seen his face—of King Renato of Anjou, and the distinguished captain of the illustrious *Coulon el Mozo*. I made myself a gentleman, and as a gentleman, I managed my intrigues more successfully than before: through stories that I invented, rumors I started myself, reports that had never been made to me, whisperings, feigned discretions, things revealed that I had promised and swore I would never tell another soul, letters half read, imaginary projects that called me away to other courts, I made the Aragonese and the Castilian think that there was another player in the game—with the help of a doctor and astrologer who was more of a troublemaker than Beelzebub, whom I had the good luck to win to my cause—a player who threatened to win away from this kingdom, thanks to the foolish incredulity of some and the foolish blindness of others, a fabulous undertaking whose immense profits other, better-advised sovereigns, had already recognized . . . And that was how I unexpectedly found myself, by royal command, seated on a well-harnessed black-and-white mule trotting down the road, trot, trot, trot, trying not to get too much dust on my only decent suit, going toward the enormous encampment at Santa Fe, the huge military caravansary that the Royal Presences were using as a capital, where, amid sumptuous cloth pavilions and patched quilt tents, bivouac fires, plates of grilled fish in wagons hung with silk awnings, bags of red wine carried by burros, guitar flourishes and the staccato heel-beats of dancing whores, trumpet calls and percussive volleys, the troops would depart to break the blockade of a long siege, dealing the death blow to the last bastion of Mohammed in this country, where — to repeat a widely known fact — there is no shortage of renegades of every stripe, Moslem mothers and daughters who had taken up with Christians, having been picked up who knows where, the way King Alphonse VI, before fornicating with his sister Doña Urraca — such families, my Lord! — picked up the notorious Zaida, whom he kept for a long time as his concubine, that broad-hipped, high-breasted Moor from Toledo whose skin smelled of marzipan, the candy sold in the shape of the serpent in the Garden, with green sugar eyes and a tongue of colored taffy, coiled up in a round box all embroidered in gold.

That was in July. I had just turned forty. Without claiming to be a handsome man, I felt I struck a good figure, with noble features and a Roman nose, clear eyes, my speech fluid and my gestures manly, my face smooth, and my skin unweathered by the marine air and the African sun, though my hair had already turned gray — which gave me a certain dignity, in addition to conveying an impression of experience and good judgment, attributed as it is, though often mistakenly, to something that merely marks the passage of the years. It was hot when I reached Santa Fe.

he too had just turned forty. And, excusing the absence of her husband, who was busy with matters of great importance—actually, questions of wine, women, and falconry—she received me by herself, in her private room, amid Moorish furniture inlaid with mother-of-pearl, which they had left behind in their retreat to Granada. It had been five years since I had seen her, in an unsatisfactory interview during which she had been peevish and inattentive and had seemed to me almost odious. But that time her headdress, with its veil that encircled her head, kept me from noticing that she was fair-haired and fair-skinned, like some Venetian women; her blue-green eyes were remarkably beautiful in a face so smooth and pink that it appeared that of a much younger woman, a face marked by an ironic and willful smile, owing perhaps to the many victories that her acute intelligence had produced in days of political discord and momentous decisions. She was no longer—as most people knew—a queen enamored of a man unworthy of such sentiment, since he had deceived her, in the sight and knowledge of his servants, with any maid of honor, woman of the court, saucy waiting maid, or attractive kitchen servant who happened to pass before him—when he wasn't occupied with some converted Moor, hot-blooded Jew, or woman of the troops, if there was no better flesh in which to sink his teeth. Now the person to whom I was speaking of my great project was—as everyone also knew—the one who truly governed. The one who had followed the chancellor into the cathedral in Segovia, on the day of her coronation, brandishing a sword erect as a man's member, grasped by the point, as a symbol of sovereignty and justice—and how they

65

had criticized such a display of machisma!—now was the one who managed all the affairs of state with such energy. The Aragonese did nothing—except where his pack of hunting dogs was concerned, of course—without her consent. He had to show her his resolutions and decrees, and even his own letters, which she passed judgment on with such authority that if one of them displeased her she had it torn up by a secretary in the presence of her husband, whose orders—and everyone knew it—didn't count for much, even in Aragon and Catalonia, whereas everyone across the country quaked in fear at the commands of the one who was the more vigorous, lively, intelligent, courageous, and wise of the two . . . In my first interview with that woman who had been born in Madrigal de las Altas Torres (and later I would have ample reason to love the name of that town), I spoke as I always did before the great and the powerful; once again I displayed my bag of wonders, my hallelujahs of dazzling geographies, but, as I began my recitation of possible marvels, a new idea began to take shape, based on my recent readings, and it seemed to delight my audience. Basing my argument on the concept of universal history developed by Paulus Orosius, I maintained that as the movement of the heavens and the stars is from east to west, so also the rule of the world has passed from the Assyrians to the Medes, from the Medes to the Persians, and then to the Macedonians, and then to the Romans, and then to the Gauls and the Germans, and finally to the Goths, founders of these reigns. It was fitting, therefore, that when the Moors had been driven from Granada—something that would soon be accomplished—we should look to the west, following the traditional expansion of the realms, governed by the movement of the stars, to reach the great and true empires of Asia—the Portuguese, after all, had only reached the outlying vassal states in their navigations along the Levantine routes. Naturally, I invoked Seneca's prophesy, with such success that my royal listener arrogantly interrupted me to recite, from memory, some verses from the tragedy:

Haec cum femineo constitit in choro,
unius facies praenitet omnibus

Kneeling before her, I repeated those verses, assuring her that she was the one of whom the great poet had been thinking when he said that "when she appeared from amid the chorus of women" — of all the women in the world — "all the others' faces paled beside hers." She gave me a slight but thrilling wink at that, and had me get up and sit next to her, and bit by bit we began to piece together the beautiful tragedy from memory . . . And that day, moved by the audacity of the woman who had thought me incapable of it, words came from me as if spoken by another — words that I will not repeat in my confession — until I was called from the room by the camp reveille beginning to sound. And ever since that happy day there has been only one woman for me in the world, the world that still waited *for me* to be fulfilled.

But the world was impatient to be fulfilled. And the most impatient of all was me, newly embroiled in arguments, controversies, reflections, demonstrations, sophistries, discussions — all crap! — of cosmographies, geographies, theologies, for those whom I was trying to convince of the validity and great profitability of my enterprise, although as always, as always, as always, without revealing my great secret: what Master Jacob had revealed to me in the diurnal nights of the Land of Ice. To have spoken of that — and more than once, from pure exasperation, I was on the point of doing so — would have refuted my most argumentative opponents. But then the aspirer to the World Atlas could have been any sailor, more a student of taverns than of Pavía, more a cheesemonger than a pilot of *Coulon el Mozo* — and then we would see if in the end it didn't fall to someone else to command the fleet that I wanted for myself! Several months passed, Granada finally fell, the Jews were expelled from Spain — *Hey, Jews, better pack your bags!* — and everything was glorious for the double crown, but I remained in the doldrums . . . In the nights of our intimacy, *Columba* — as I called her when we were alone — promised me three caravels, ten caravels, fifty caravels, a hundred caravels, all the caravels I wanted; but, at daybreak, the caravels went up in smoke, and I was alone, walking at dawn, going home, watching the masts and sails that had been triumphantly erected in my visions of grandeur being lowered, returned, in the light of day, to the shadowy unreality of dreams that never come true . . . And so I began to ask myself whether my destiny was not to end up as no more than the object of the queen's affections, like Don Martín Vásquez de Arce, the tender and gentle page of Sigüenza, who had perished in bizarre combat against the Moors because of his determination to prove his valor before his Dame — the inspirer of his labors and guide of his passions. (And how jealous I was, at times, of that young soldier poet to whom in my trials of love I perhaps attributed better fortune than he actually received from the one who never mentioned him, perhaps because he was so pleasing, so enormously pleasing, that she feared I would read in her eyes her preference for him!) Such torments afflict those of the race of common glass when they mingle with those of diamond! . . .

I had seen the royal standard raised over the towers of the Alhambra; I had been present at the humiliation of the Moorish king, wrested from his vanquished city and made to kiss the hands of my monarchs. And now they were hatching grander schemes: now they were talking about carrying the war to Africa. But all I heard was, We'll see, we'll think about it, we'll talk about it, it's better to wait a while, because there's always another day, and patience is a great virtue, better the evil we know than the evil we don't know . . . I had raised a million maravedis from the Genoans of Seville and the banker Berardi.

But I still needed another million to set to sea. And it was this other million that Columba promised me every evening only to take it back at daybreak—she didn't even have to say so—when she told me "time to go" and bade me farewell. But one night I blew up. I was seized by a rapidly mounting fury, and I shouted at the top of my voice that as deferential and submissive as I had been to her, mindful that a royal purple, even if it's invisible, always cloaks the body of a queen, still I felt that I was the equal of any monarch and was just as important, for though I lacked a jeweled crown, I wore the aura of my great idea, the way they wore the crowns of Castile and Aragón. "Pig!" she screamed at me. "You're nothing but a pig!" "Pig yourself!" I shouted back. "And you know better than anyone what I am and what I have been!" And then I could no longer keep the secret I had carried for years, and I told her what I had heard in Ice Land about the voyages of the redhead and his son Leif and their discovery of Green Land and Wood Land and Vinland; I told her about the marvelous country of fir trees, wheat fields, waters shimmering with salmon; I described the manikins with their gold necklaces, gold bracelets, gold breastplates, gold helmets, and I told her how they also worshipped golden idols, and I said that in their rivers gold was as plentiful as pebbles on the Spanish plain . . . And in the face of Columba's astonished silence, I shouted that I was going away and never coming back and that I would offer my great enterprise to the king of France, who was anxious to finance it, because he was one king who had an intelligent wife, a queen who was drawn to the sea like a good Breton, worthy descendant of Hélène of Armorica, daughter of King Clohel, wife of Constantine the Elder, who had been chosen by the Lord to exhume the Cross, which was buried twenty hands underground in Mount Golgotha in Jerusalem. One can count on people like them, and so I'm going to take my proposition to them! . . . This seemed to infuriate Columba: "Pig! Filthy swine! You would betray Christ for thirty denarii!" she screamed, as I left the room, slamming the door behind me. Outside, hitched to some trees, my good dappled mule was waiting for me. Angrier than I could remember ever having been before — and doubly so for having let out the great secret that I ought to have kept to myself — I rode a good two leagues before I stopped at a tavern, intending to drink as much wine as my belly would hold. It was the beginning of April. In the sunlight, the green of the fields took on the orange tint that is peculiar to the vegetation of Granada. The finches were singing. There was a wild scene in the tavern, which was already filled despite the early hour, with peasants enjoying their Sunday. The bells of the church were calling the faithful to Mass. But I was in a black mood; each glass instead of lifting my spirits threw me deeper into the despair of one who has committed an irredeemable error. I had lost everything. Everything. The favor of the queen and the hope that had at least been alive a few hours before, even if it hadn't been realized. And I had drained a pitcher of wine when I saw a constable come in, who, to judge from his sweat-drenched, filthy uniform, must have ridden hard to get here. He headed straight for me as soon as he saw me: Her Majesty asked me to return to her at once, begging me to give up my journey . . . A little after midday, having washed my face and changed my clothes, I appeared before my royal Mistress. "You have the million maravedis," she told me. She had gotten them from the banker Santángel using the persuasiveness that I knew so well. As collateral she had given him some jewels that were actually worth much less. "I'll take them back when I please," she said, "and without returning the million." She gave me a hard look. "We have expelled the Jews. It's worth a million for Santángel to remain in this country where his business is so good. So now, pack *your* bags! Good luck. And send all the gold you can so we can carry on the war in Africa." "And even reconquer the city of Jerusalem the way we have reconquered the kingdom of Granada," I said. "Perhaps," she replied. "But tell no one about my great secret," I said, suddenly alarmed at the thought that Santángel might have been informed about what . . . "I am not that stupid!" she said. "In that secret is glory for both of us." "The Holy Spirit has inspired you," I said, kissing her hands. "Perhaps that is what future books will say," she said. "Of course, those books will be written only if you discover something." "So you still have doubts?" "*Alea jacta est* . . ." Outside I heard the shouts of a Moorish water vendor, dressed in a tasseled hat and a coat of many colors that barely covered his balls; he was praising the freshness of the bags of water that hung around his neck and was so absorbed in his business of pouring out streams of water that he kept at it as if the Kingdom of Granada had not changed rulers.

n the third day of August at eight o'clock in the morning, we left the Bar of Saltés. A strong sea wind bore us sixty miles to the south, which is fifteen leagues; then southwest and south by west, which was the course for the Canary Islands . . . Little of interest or importance occurred until the sixth of September, when we set sail from the island of Gomera. Now our great adventure began. I forced myself to put the best face on things throughout the voyage, always to appear pleased with the way things were going, but I have to admit that at night, when I tried to sleep, I found that I couldn't. I grappled until dawn with the difficulties that lay ahead on this hazardous voyage to far-off Vinland — or to the land that lay to the south of it — which I had described to my Mistress as a province, based on the reports I had received, of a kingdom ruled by the Grand Khan or some other prince of the Indies, for whom she had given me letters; and, in case my invention turned out to be true, I had brought aboard ship a certain Luis de Torres, who "used to be" a Jew (this "used to be" was often heard in those days), and who said he knew not only Hebrew but also Aramaic and a little Arabic. But I had drawn a bad crew. They were recently baptized Christians, criminals fleeing justice, circumcised men about to be thrown out of the country, rogues and adventurers, rather than men of the sea who knew how to raise the sail and luff with the wind, who had experience manning these ships. They did the ship's work poorly, they executed my commands poorly. And I knew that if the voyage took much longer than I had projected — which could easily happen — the men, aware that with each passing day they were farther from the continent they had left behind, unable to see land ahead (and they were all anxious to see it, since the crown had offered a reward of ten thousand maravedis to the man who gave the first alert), would be easy prey to discouragement, disobedience, and the desire to turn back. In many minds the image of the dark ocean was still very much alive, an image of endless seas, of currents dragging ships irresistibly toward the point where the waves meet the sky, endless seas that had been identified for centuries with the very waters we were passing through, so that if we took too long those images would flood the sailors' minds, weakening their wills and tempting them to insurrection. So I resorted to a lie, a deception, the constant fiction I had promulgated since Sunday, the ninth of September (and this I will tell the confessor), which was to record fewer leagues than we had actually traveled, so that the crew would not be shocked or alarmed if the voyage went on too long. And so, this Monday, having gone sixty leagues, I said we had gone forty-eight. And likewise on Tuesday — a calm day — I counted twenty and said sixteen. At first I had lowered the figure by three or four a day. But as the month wore on, noticing a growing anxiety on the faces of my crew, I began to subtract more and more leagues from the true total we had traveled. By the eighteenth, fifty-five had become forty-eight . . . And on the first of October, my real total was seven hundred and twenty leagues, whereas I showed a highly fictitious count of only five hundred eighty-four . . . It was true that we encountered unusual vegetation, which might have floated away from islands ahead of us, things like pine sprigs, or yellow-green plants like floating bunches of grapes — but grapes that looked more like mastic berries. We also saw birds overhead that could have come from land, such as pelicans and petrels, and some that were white like seagulls, and others that seemed to belong to the frigate family, all of which I greeted with wild demonstrations of joy. But many of the crew members said that these birds didn't prove a thing, that each winter storks flew over the Mediterranean, leaving German realms where they would have been exposed to snow and storms, seeking sunlit Arabian minarets. Not only that, but there are birds that can sleep on the waves, and even nest and hatch their eggs in the middle of the ocean, as is the habit of the alcyone bird. And there was grumbling and plotting among the men. As the days passed, fear spread from caravel to caravel. Treachery that started on one ship quickly passed to another, leaping from ship to ship as if by magic — and I have no doubt that the ones who started the worst talk were the ones with some education, the sad fact being that insolent talk, petty gossip, and even slander sprang up like weeds among the men who had some learning and thought they knew it all, who seemed to take particular pleasure in sharpening their tongues on others' backs, especially if the other was the one who gave the orders. I suspected that Rodrigo de Torres, who called himself a doctor; and the new Christian Luis de Torres, who claimed to speak Chaldean and Arabic; and even the loud-mouthed Andalusian Martín Alonso, in whom I had placed so much confidence, but whom I was beginning to like less and less, were the three who started spreading the story that I didn't really know how to use an astrolabe — which might have been true years ago, I have to admit, when I made a serious error in determining the latitude of the kingdom of Mina in Africa. (But, I repeat, that was years before.) They also said, when they got together in their slanderous circles, that the map drawn by Toscanelli that I kept in my cabin wasn't good for anything but was just for show, since I was incapable of following the mathematics of that lofty thinker — which might have been true, but I had reconciled myself to that long ago, knowing that Toscanelli, so proud of his science, had invalidated the mathematics of Nicholas of Cusa, the friend of Pope Pius II, whose *Historia rerum* held the place of honor among my books. (As for me — and this is something the Spaniards who were traveling with me could not understand, those men who were too smart by half, philosophers of the tar brush and the caulk pot, great thinkers of seawater and tuna fish — I felt that if Nicholas of Cusa was weak in mathematics, as the pedantic Toscanelli claimed, he remained the proponent of the *docta ignorantia,* which I hold as my own: the *docta ignorantia* that easily open the doors to the infinite, in contrast to scholastic logic, with its ferrules and mortarboards, which puts blinders, gags, and earmuffs on bold thinkers, seers, the gatekeepers of the ideal, the true *cephalophoros,* eager to transcend the limits of the unknown . . .) And, not content to turn the crew against me with their slanders and lies, those rogues insinuated that I had confused the Arabic miles of Alfagán with the Italian miles I employed. This last accusation, despite the vexation it caused me, began to seem true, a source of private embarrassment, since, despite having intentionally falsified my daily account of our movements by mixing up the miles, as those shit-assed Spaniards claimed, I had gravely underestimated the earth's circumference, which meant that the trip would take much longer than expected, to the great consternation and apprehension of my crew.

On the ninth of October I received intelligence that unrest was spreading like magic on board the ships. The following day the sailors came to tell me — first in a pleading tone, then with words that grew more and more forceful, stronger and stronger, until they bordered on insolence — that such a long voyage could not be endured, that they were worried, that the biscuits and jerky were running out, that many men had taken sick, that their spirits were low and they had no will to continue, and that it was time to abandon this endless quest, which wasn't doing anyone any good. Applying all my energy and the same eloquence I had shown in my discussions with sovereigns, theologians, and philosophers, as well as the threat of the gallows — though I didn't linger on that but only hinted at it indirectly, meta-phorically — which I directed at the rudest and most unruly among them, I quickly painted such a picture of wealth and profit, pointing at the horizon, asking them to continue looking for land for just three or four more days, that I finally managed to ride out the storm of voices on which I was tossed, under the cunning gaze of Martín Alonso — every day I liked him less — who said to me, "Hang them, hang them," knowing that if I decided to have anyone hanged none of the sailors would carry out the order — least of all the accursed Galicians and Biscayans that it was my misfortune to have brought with me — and that I would immediately lose all my authority, command, and dignity (which was probably precisely what Martín Alonso wanted) . . . Still, I knew that from then on the days of my voyage were numbered. If something extraordinary did not happen tomorrow, the day after tomorrow, or the day after that, I would have to return to Castile in such a misery of broken dreams that I didn't dare to imagine the greeting I would receive, and rightly so, from a scowling Madrigal of the High Towers, who, when she was angry could command the vocabulary of a teamster, modeling her style on the Moors, cursing and blaspheming a person's maternal ancestors back for five generations . . . But the extraordinary thing occurred, when my crew fished out of the water a little piece of wood that had been curiously worked by a human hand. And the men on the *Niña* found a small stick covered with tiny seasnails. We were all hopeful, anxious, expectant. Some of the men said they could smell land. At ten that night I thought I could discern lights in the distance. To confirm this I called the comptroller Rodrigo Sánchez and the king's steward, who saw them too . . . And at two on Friday morning Rodrigo de Triana sang out, "Land! Land!" which was like the music of the *Te Deum* to the rest of us . . . We immediately lowered the sails, except for the mainsail, and we lay to, waiting for daybreak. But now our joy was mixed with speculation, because we didn't know what we would find. An island? Terra firma? Had we, in fact, reached the Indies? And every sailor knows that there are three Indies:

those of Cathay and Cipango, in addition to the Greater Indies—the Golden Chersonese of the ancients?—besides the many lesser states that produce spices. (As for me, I was also concerned about the danger posed by the fierce and warlike manikins.) No one could sleep now that we had arrived, thinking about the many risks, such as fatal diseases, that might await us on the shore where we could see bonfires burning. So Rodrigo de Triana came to me to claim the silk doublet that had been promised as a reward to the man who first saw land. I gave it to him with pleasure, yet the sailor stood there as if expecting something more. Then, after a silence, he reminded me of the reward of ten thousand maravedis the king and queen had promised in addition to the doublet. "You will see that when we return," I said. "But . . ." "What?" "Couldn't Your Mercy, my Admiral, advance me a little now on account?" "Why?" "For the whores, by your leave . . . I haven't had a screw in fifty days." "And who says there are whores in these lands?" "Where there are sailors, there are always whores." "They don't use money here; as I understand it, according to the accounts of the Venetian Marco Polo, in these countries, they pay for everything with pieces of paper the size of your hand that are stamped with the mark of the Great Khan." Saddened, Rodrigo went off with his doublet thrown over his shoulder . . . As for his reward of ten thousand maravedis (and this I will have to tell the confessor), he could keep on waiting—and he'd better be careful not to ask for it too loud or make too much of a fuss about it, since I knew some things about him that he might not want anyone else to know—because I'd already earmarked it for Beatriz, my good-looking Biscayan woman, whom I'd given a son but not a wedding ring, and who had been in tears for a long time because of my remoteness and neglect, which were the result of the royal favor that had been granted me, an overflowing cornucopia: three ships ready to weigh anchor; the humiliation of my enemies; the thrill of discovering new routes; the glory of being here, tonight, waiting for the appearance of the sun, which is slow, so slow—so goddamned slow—to appear; and perhaps immortality, to be remembered as the man who, starting from humble beginnings, now could claim the title of Magnifier of the World . . . No, Rodrigo! Go screw yourself! I'm keeping your ten-thousand-maravedi reward! . . . I too could have shouted "Land!" when I saw the flickering lights, but I didn't. I could have shouted it out before you did, but I didn't. And I didn't because, having made out land and put an end to my worries, I couldn't raise my voice like a simple sentry anxious to win such a petty prize for such a sudden glory. The doublet that you carried off, Rodrigo, would have been too little for a man who had instantly become Atlas the giant; a reward of ten thousand maravedis was too little, unworthy of my newly realized destiny, so I would deliver it into the hands of *she whom I command,* that swollen woman, pregnant at last with the offspring of the man who has just acquired the stature of Herald, Seer, Discoverer. I am who I am, like the Lord of Wrath, and from this moment on I can call myself *Don,* because from this moment on—all must recognize and say it—I am the Grand Admiral of the Ocean Sea and Viceroy and Perpetual Governor of All the Islands and Terra Firma that I have discovered and that henceforth, following my command, will be discovered and won in the Ocean Sea.

ours of great uneasiness and uncertainty. Interminable as this night feels to me, soon, just the same, must come the dawn — strangely delayed, it seems to me. I have dressed in my finest garments, as all the Spaniards aboard the ships are doing. From the great shield, I have taken the royal banner, mounting it on a lance, and I have done the same for the banners of the green cross that my two captains will carry — tremendous sons of bitches they have proven to be — which ostentatiously display, beneath their corresponding crowns embroidered in silk, the initials *F* and *Y* — the latter especially pleasing to me, since, together with the five letters that complete the name *Ysabel,* it becomes for me the almost present image of the person to whom I owe my election and investiture. But now there is a great movement of Spaniards on deck: bronzes that roll and crawl, irons that collide with each other. And that's because I have commanded the lombards and cannons to be made ready for what is to come. We will all, moreover, be armed when we land, because any conjecture formed in this period of waiting might prove valid. There are people not far from us — because where there are no people there are no bonfires. But I find it impossible to form an opinion on the nature of these people. Not only have I studied Marco Polo, whose stories of his travels I have annotated with my hand and mark, but I have also read Juan de Monte Corvino — though I never found the occasion to cite him in my discourses — who also left from Venice and traveled to the glorious city of Cambaluc, the Grand Khan's capital, where he not only built a Christian church with three bell towers but also performed six thousand baptisms, translated the Psalms into the Tartar tongue, and even founded a choir of boys who devoted their sweet voices to singing the praises of the Lord. There he encountered Oderico de Pordenone — another whom I know well — who had been made a full archbishop, with a church that had grown into a cathedral, with acolytes and suffragans, many of whom wanted to be sent out as missionaries, since the people of that country were wonderfully tolerant — they rejoiced in their tolerance — and accepted any religion so long as it did not affect the interests of the state — a tolerance that, certainly, had spread a vexing proliferation of Nestorian heresies, whose abominable faults, in his time, the eminent doctor of Seville had already denounced in his *Etimilogías* . . . So it was not impossible that the catechizing of Juan de Monte Corvino had reached as far as these shores — through the work of the Franciscans, men of vast travels! . . . In that case, Christopher, Christobalillo, you who invented during this voyage the name *Christo-phoros,* transporter of Christ, bearer of Christ, Saint Christopher, reading yourself into the most famous and important texts of the Faith, as you had always been inclined to do, assigning yourself the role of Predestined One, Unique and Necessary Man — a sacred mission — you who offered your enterprise to the highest bidder, finally selling yourself for a million maravedis; in that case, deluded imposter, you would have no choice but to raise the sails again, steer close by the wind, and use the small sail with the *Niña, Pinta, Santa María,* and all to die of shame at the feet of your Mistress of the High Towers. In this cowardly hour — the third hour — you consider, disoriented sailor, since the very point of the compass turns away from you toward the north, that the worst thing that could happen to you would be that the Gospels might shy from you if they were found. It is true that, by the will of your Mistress, you had been hastily admitted to the Franciscan order so that you were authorized to wear the cowl-less sackcloth of the mendicants. But . . . what will you do, poor ostiary, medi- ocre reader, unapproved exorcist and acolyte, in the face of a deacon, a bishop who raises his hand and says to you: "Go back, you're not needed here." So you hope, yes, you hope, that the Gospels will not have traveled the way of your caravels. The war of the Word against the Word. The Word traveling from the east, which will have to rise early and meet the west. Absurd stubbornness that could kill me, my body as well as my work. An uneven battle, since I don't carry the Gospels on board — I don't even have a chaplain, who at least could recite them. Against the Evangelists, should they stand in my way, I would fire lombards and cannons, if that were possible. But no: under their capes of gold inlaid with precious stones they scoff at such nonsense. If the Rome of the Caesars could not handle them, how could this poor sailor waiting anxiously for the dawn, for the hour when the light of the world would reveal whether his enterprise has been futile or whether it will gain him everlasting glory. If Matthew, Mark, Luke, and John are waiting for me on that nearby beach, I'm screwed. I lose the chance of being *Christophoros* for posterity and have to return to the Savona tavern. If only I can find an abundance of spices. The rich dance of Doña Cinnamon with Don Clove. But I have said that the Grand Khan rules here. And his people, already corrupted by our commerce, are not going to give away pepper or myrrh but are going to demand a good price, not the trinkets I bought at the eleventh hour and brought along for barter. And as for gold and pearls, they'll be even less disposed to give those away than the ginger, which Juan de Monte Corvino described so well, comparing it to gladioli roots . . . My Spaniards chant and sing a *Salve,* at once impatient and uneasy — although for other reasons than I — now that the sea adventure has ended and the land adventure begun . . . And suddenly it is dawn: a dawn that almost seems to fall upon us, so rapidly does the brightness ascend, a portentous light unlike any I have ever seen in other lands I have visited. I scrutinize the horizon. There are no buildings, houses, castles, towers, or battlements to be seen. No cross appears above the trees. So, it would seem, there are no churches. There are no churches. So far I have not heard the dreaded sound of a bell forged of solid bronze . . . Only the welcome sound of our oars moving a marvelously calm and clear water, in whose sandy depths I make out the presence of huge conch shells in unfamiliar shapes. Now my anxiety is transformed into jubilation. And now we are on the land, where we cannot recognize the trees, except for some palms that resemble those of Africa. As soon as we concluded the formalities of taking possession and the corresponding establishment and testimony of the Faith — which the secretary, Rodrigo de Escobedo, did not complete, since he was startled by the sound of voices in the bushes — the leaves parted, and we found ourselves surrounded by people. After our initial fright, many of us began to laugh, because the people who approached us were naked, with barely even a handkerchief to cover their shame. And we had put on our breastplates, chain mail, and helmets, in anticipation of a possible assault from tremendous warriors with weapons raised! . . . These people had no arms, except for spears resembling oxherds' goads, and I felt that they must be miserable people, very miserable, tremendously miserable, since they went naked — or nearly so — as the day they were born, even a young woman whose exposed breasts were studied by my men, who wanted to touch them, with a lust that raised my fury, and I was forced to cry out in an inappropriate manner, unable to maintain the solemn demeanor appropriate to one bearing the standard of Their Highnesses. Some of the natives carried green parrots that did not speak, perhaps from fright, and balls of cotton thread — not as fine, certainly, as those obtained in other parts of the Indies. And they exchanged everything for some things that weren't worth a fig, which we had brought along onshore in anticipation of possible trade: small glass beads, hawks' bells — hawks' bells that they especially liked to hold to their ears to hear them better — rings of brass, along with the many colored caps I had bought in the markets of Seville, when I remembered, on the eve of weighing anchor, that the manikins of Vinland were extremely fond of colored cloth and fabric. In exchange for these trifles, they gave us their parrots and cotton; unarmed, they seemed to be peaceful people, who would make humble and obedient servants — neither black nor white, they were more the color of the people of the Canary Islands, with straight hair, thick and flowing as the manes of horses. We did no more that day, excited as we were by the discovery and taking possession of the island and the desire for rest, after a sleepless night. "Where have we arrived, Admiral?" asked Martín Alonso, with venom concealed beneath a smiling mask. "The main thing is, we have arrived," I replied . . . And now, back on board the lead ship, I looked upward, exulting in legitimate pride before the scoundrels who just a few days before had raised their voices — and even their fists — at me, on the verge of mutiny — and not just the Andalusians but almost all the caulkers, carpenters, coopers, who came on board; not so much the Jews who by having come with me had been saved from expulsion; not so much the new Christians who too often turned toward Mecca at nightfall, as the accursed, ungovernable, obstinate, disrespectful Biscayans who formed a clique around Juan de la Cosa, so full of his knowledge of cartography, always talking up his *science* (as I had learned from the other title-bearer, Vicente Yáñez, just as treacherous as Martín Alonso, but a better captain . . .) trying to prove that I was a mariner with nothing but bluster and ambition, a navigator of palace bedrooms who mixed up his latitudes and confused different measures of maritime miles, who was unable to successfully conclude this kind of enterprise.

. . . Now small bells are ringing, lingering in the thin drizzle that dampens the roofs of the city where my shadow has taken shelter, the protagonist of my own extinguishing light. A bleating flock passes through the street. And still the confessor has not come. And even though it is May, there is an autumnal light that tears me from the resplendent islands where—perhaps because I had not taken a chaplain aboard the ships, perhaps because I had never thought of converting or indoctrinating anyone—the devil waited to catch me in his traps. And the evidence of those traps is here, in the draft of my account of my voyages that I keep under my pillow, and that I pull out now with trembling hand—terrified by myself—to reread what, in my final moments, seems an entire repertoire of illusions—as I will tell my confessor who is so slow in arriving. A repertoire of illusions that began on October thirteenth with the word GOLD. Because that Saturday I returned to the newly dis-covered island in the hope of seeing what I could obtain from it besides cotton balls and parrots—already we didn't know what to do with all the parrots that were covering the wooden decks with layer upon layer of white birdshit—when I saw, with a thrill of surprise, that some of the Indians (we began to call them *Indians,* since we were probably in the outer reaches of the West Indies) wore small bits of gold in their noses. I said: GOLD. Seeing this marvel, I felt a sort of internal shock. A lust the likes of which I had never known rumbled in my gut. My hands trembled. Shaken, sweating, determined, crazed, peppering these men with sign-language questions, I tried to find out about the source of the gold, how they had obtained it, where it was found, how it was mined, how it was worked, since it seemed that they had no iron tools or crucibles. And I felt the metal, appraised its weight, bit it, tested it, burnished it with a handkerchief to look at it in the sun, examining it in the sunlight, making it shine in that light, taking the gold and putting it in my palm, verifying that it was gold, pure gold, true gold—the gold standard. And the ones who wore it, astonished, seized and shaken by their rings like oxen by their noses, separated from the others by virtue of that prize, made me to understand that there lay to the south another island with a great king who had pots of gold. And not only was there gold in that kingdom but precious stones as well. Now, from their description, that sounded more like Cipango than Vinland. And so, impelled by the evil spirit who suddenly lodged in my soul, I turned to violence, ordering seven of those men taken prisoner, and we bound and placed them in the hold, paying no mind to their cries and laments or to the protests of the others, whom I held back with my sword—and they knew, having felt one of our blades, that our swords cut deep and caused their blood to gush . . . We returned to the sea on Sunday, the day of our Lord, with no pity for the tears of the captives whom we had berthed in the prow so that they could guide us. And from that day on, GOLD was the word most often repeated in my diaries, reports, and letters. But there was little gold in the islands we had discovered so far, all full of naked men and women who wore only—as I wrote Their Highnesses—"little scraps of cotton that barely covered their sex"—where my eyes strayed at times, I must admit, like the eyes of my Spaniards—so much, so much, that I had to threaten them with punishment if, with their flies so swollen, they gave way to their lust. If I could contain myself, they could do the same! We didn't come here to fuck but to find gold, the gold that was beginning to appear, that was showing up on every island; the gold that led us on, that was our guiding light, the great compass that directed our travels. And to be sure we were on the right path to the gold, we kept on giving out red caps, hawks' bells, and other trifles—and I was proud to boast of the inequity of those exchanges to our Rulers!—that weren't worth so much as a maravedi, although we obtained many bits of the coveted bright metal for them. But I was not satisfied with gold torn from noses and ears, because now they were telling me about the great land of Cobla or Cuba, where it seemed there were both gold and pearls, as well as spices: so we traveled there, arriving on Sunday, the day of our Lord.

I was sincere when I wrote that this land seemed to me the most beautiful that human eyes had ever seen. It was fertile, hilly, varied, substantial, thickly forested, rich in vegetation — more extensive vegetation, with taller palm trees, fuller rivers, higher uplands and deeper valleys than we had seen before on islands that seemed to me, I confess, like crazy islands, floating, sleepwalking, having little to do with the maps and texts that had nourished me. I had to describe that new land. But when I tried to do so, I was halted by the perplexity of one who tries to name things totally different from what is known — things that must have names, since things that have no names cannot be imagined, but whose names I did not know, and I was not another Adam, chosen by Christ to name the things of the world. I could make up words, certainly; but the words would *not reveal the thing,* if the thing were not already known. To designate a table, when someone says *table,* it is necessary that there be, in the mind of the one who hears, a *table-concept,* with the appropriate qualities of *table-ness.* But here, before this admirable landscape that I gazed upon, only the word *palm* had a referential value, since there are palms in Africa, palms — though different from the ones here — are found in many places, and, consequently, the word *palm* is accompanied by a clear image — and especially for those who know the religious significance of Palm Sunday. On Sunday we reached this place, and the memorializing quill remained motionless after recording the four letters of the word *palm.* A rhetorician, perhaps, who handles the Castilian language better than I, a poet, perhaps, using similes and metaphors, might have accomplished more, and succeeded in describing what I could not: those trees, all tangled together, their forms new to me: that one, whose leaves are gray in back and green in front, which, when they fall and dry, curl up on themselves like hands around a rope; that other, reddish, whose trunk grows by shedding transparent skins like moulting snakes; that one farther on, solitary and monumental, in the

middle of a small clearing, with its boughs extending horizon-
tally like a necklace around a thick, bristly trunk, looking like a
rostrate column . . . And the fruits: that one, with a drab brown
rind and a red flesh, with a seed like carved mahogany; that
other, with violet flesh, its seeds inside a gelatin paste; that other,
larger, smaller, never the same as the one next to it, with a
fragrant, white, bittersweet center, always fresh and juicy even in
the midday heat . . . All new, unique, pleasing despite their
difference, but so far nothing very useful. Neither Doña
Nutmeg nor Doña Pepper nor Doña Cinnamon nor Doña
Cardamom had appeared anywhere. As for gold, they said that it
was found in abundance. And I thought that it was time for that
divine metal to show up, since now that its existence on these
islands had been demonstrated, a new problem possessed me:
the three caravels represented a debt of two million. I wasn't
particularly concerned about Santángel's million, because monarchs settle their debts when and how they please, and as for
Columba's jewels, they were jewels from the back of the jewel
box and, tough-minded though she could be when she chose,
she was not yet ready to call for them back, so soon after the
expulsion of the Jews. But there remained the other million: the
million from the Genoans of Seville, who would make my life
impossible if I returned empty-handed . . . For the moment, I
bided my time: *This country is the most beautiful that human eyes
have ever seen* . . . and so we continued, refining our panegyric.
As for the landscape, I didn't have to rack my brain: I say that the
blue mountains I can see in the distance are like those of Sicily,
though they are nothing like those of Sicily. I say that the grass is
as tall as that of Andalusia in April and May, though there is
nothing here that is anything like Andalusia. I say nightingales
are singing when I hear twittering little gray birds with long,
black beaks that are more like sparrows. I allude to the fields of
Castile, here where not a single thing recalls the fields of Castile.
I have seen no spice trees, and I suggest that there may be spices

here. I speak of *gold mines* where I know of none. I speak of pearls, many pearls, merely because I see some mussels that "signal their presence." I say only one thing that is true: that the dogs here seem not to bark. But with dogs that don't even know how to bark I am not going to pay back the million that I owe to the accursed Genoans of Seville, who are capable of sending your mother to the galleys for a debt of fifty maravedis. And the worst of all is that I don't have the slightest idea where I am; this land of Colba or Cuba could just as well be the southern extreme of Vinland as an eastern shore of Cipango—keeping in mind that there are three Indies. I have said that this is a continent, terra firma, of infinite size. Juan de la Cosa, who is always around, and who no matter what I say says the opposite, insists that it is an island. I don't know what to think. But I say it's a continent, and that should suffice—after all, I'm the admiral, and I know what I'm talking about. He talks about sailing around the island, and I say that since it is not an island we will not sail around it. The bastard . . . That's enough! I pick up my quill again and resume my repertoire of good news, my catalog of brilliant prognostications. And I assure my readers—I assure myself—that soon I will be looking into the face of the Grand Khan. (The name of the *Grand Khan* resonates of gold, gold dust, gold bars, gold treasure chests, gold casks: the sweet music of gold coins clattering, spilling onto the banker's table: celestial music . . .)

realized very quickly that the country they called Cuba would not be the place where I would finally see the magnificent, impassive face of the Grand Khan. I dispatched two able messengers to see if there was an important city or fortress here (Luis de Torres, who, as I have said, spoke Hebrew, Arabic, and Aramaic, and Rodrigo de Jerez, who knew most of an African dialect . . .), and they both came back with the news that they had encountered only little villages with huts and Indians just like those we had already seen. There wasn't any sign of gold here. They showed the Indians the little samples of cinnamon and cloves that I had given them, but no one seemed to recognize those spices. So I still seemed far from the brilliant kingdom of Cipango. But not so far that I would give up my plan of going on blindly sailing over unknown routes, fortifying myself with the knowledge that I left behind me islands that I had christened, that I had inscribed in the geography of the world, that I had lifted from the obscurity of the barbarous idioms with which their peoples designated them, to give one the august name of Santa María de la Concepción and another the pleasing, very pleasing to me, name of Isabella. And perhaps with the thought that the account of my trip might be read some day by my Mistress, I took great pains to describe — as I never did again with any other place — the beauty of the groves of trees, the lushness of the plants, which reminds me (. . . my intended reader in mind) of the delights of an April in Andalusia, with its delicious perfumes, its fragrance of fruit; and (. . . my intended reader, once again) of *the song of the little birds,* which is so seductive that *a man never wants to leave the place . . .* But now I have to push forward, explore the coast of this Cuba, and continue my search for gold. Of the seven Indians we captured on the first island, two have escaped. And we are lying to the ones who are left (another ruse), denying our intention of taking them to Spain for display at the court and assuring them that we will return them to their country with many wonderful gifts as soon as we find a sufficient quantity of gold. They find our food repugnant and refuse to taste dried beef, or cheese, or biscuits — they will accept only fish pulled from the ocean right in front of their eyes, and even then they don't want them fried in our oil (which has gone a bit rancid), just lightly grilled over hot coals — but they have developed a taste for the wine that we carry in such quantity that people were amazed and thought I was stocking a tavern when I laid in all the casks. At first they were wary and seemed to think it was blood, but once they experienced its effects our prisoners grew quite fond of red wine, so that now they are constantly hoisting the wine pitcher I gave them and asking for more and more. The truth is that I have turned them into drunkards, night and day, because that way they stop their moaning and complaining, and when the wine has loosened their tongues they assure me that we are getting close to the gold, that we'll get to the gold any minute — and not just to gold plates and face masks and crowns and statues: to the mine, the big mine, the huge mine, where there is so much gold that my three ships won't even be able to carry it all. Juan de la Cosa has gone to his gang of Biscayans — whose language I can't understand — and Galicians — who are a bunch of foul-mouthed back-biters — and he swears to them in their nightly gatherings (I always have a spy in their midst) that the Indians have me fooled, that they are making up the stories of gold to lull my suspicions so that I will get careless, and then they'll take the first opportunity to escape, like the other two did. But we keep sailing onward, ever onward, and we are now going windward to the magnificent land of Haiti, which I call Hispaniola because of its beauty — I know what I'm doing—and if I found a city here, I will call it Isabella. But here, for the second time, I was sadly disappointed, because nothing about this newly discovered land indicated that we were getting any closer to Cipango or to a province ruled by a prince who paid taxes to the Grand Khan. And now we met some kings—who were called *caciques* here. But they were kings who didn't wear any clothes (if you can imagine such a thing!) and queens with naked breasts, and to cover their most private parts they wore nothing but a piece of cloth the size of the lace handkerchief that might be used by one of the dwarfs they have in the castles and palaces in Castile as nurses and entertainers for the infants and children of the nobility. (Courts with completely naked monarchs! Inconceivable to someone for whom the word *court* brings an immediate vision of castles, heralds, miters, and velvet robes whose purple evokes the Romans: *Regard Nero of Tarpeya / and Rome ablaze* . . .) And in front of these kings, if you can call someone a king who walks around with his private parts hanging out, I performed all the usual ceremonies: raising the flag of the Christian monarchs, cutting some boughs and leaves with my sword, three times proclaiming that I was taking possession of the land in the name of Their Highnesses, being ready—I added—to answer with my sword if anyone challenged that, and professing the Faith and saying a few prayers for Rodrigo de Escobedo, who was writing it all down; but what was exasperating, at bottom, after all my genuflections, proclamations, and arrogant challenges to combatants who never materialized, was that everything was exactly the same as before. To take possession of some part of the world, one should have to defeat an enemy, humiliate a sovereign, subjugate a people, receive the keys to a city, witness an oath of obedience. But none of those things happened here. Nothing changed. Nobody fought. Nobody seemed to pay much attention to our ceremonies and acts and proclamations. They seemed to be saying to each other—and sometimes with a maddeningly derisive smile:

"Okay, okay, no problem. For us . . . life goes on!" They gave us parrots—and we already had so many little green parrots, with sly little eyes, that had never learned how to say a single word in our language! and so many balls of cotton that already we didn't know where to store them, and some crude pots, and then they put on our red caps, took our cat-bells and dog-bells, and, looking quite funny, they burst out laughing, patting themselves on the belly. And I had taken possession of their lands without their being aware of a thing, and what was worse, without my *I claim thee* in the name of the etcetera, etcetera, etcetera (as always! . . .) procuring me any great benefit. (And so I returned to my ship, to the boat that sailed slowly past coral reefs that in the ever-changing light of this place became an undersea mirage, where everything became something else, and I could believe, seeing such a play of colors, that under that water I was seeing the magical glimmering of emeralds and diamonds, of astraean and chrysoprase from the Indies, of selenite from Persia, and even of lyncurion, which, as everyone knows, is formed by the urine of a lynx, and of draconite, which is extracted from the brain of a dragon . . . But I could only just believe it, because if I put my hand in the water and pulled until my fingers were bloody, I would acquire no greater benefit, if I managed to acquire anything at all, than to pull out a chunk of rotting seaweed . . . And, to my great disappointment, what I had taken for magnificent chrysocolla, which is found in the Asiatic countries where ants obtain gold from the ground unaided, was really only chrysopolla—and that seemed a bad joke to me.)

Five, six, seven "kings" of this island came to render tributes (or at least that was my interpretation, although the cursed Biscayans in Juan de la Cosa's circle said that they just wanted to get a look at my face . . .): kings like those we'd seen already; kings who, instead of dressing in imperial purple robes, wore a tiny codpiece for every celebration. And this procession of

naked "majesties" forced me to speculate that we were still quite
a distance from the fabulous Cipango of the Italian chronicles.
Because there they had palaces with golden roofs and courts
gleaming with gold and precious stones, and the Christian
ambassadors were received by Lords wearing golden armor,
surrounded by ministers and counselors dressed in gilded
tunics, and were served banquets on golden tablecloths while
peacocks danced the *paduana* accompanied by melodious instruments, and tame lions — like the one that became as a lapdog to
Saint Jerome — sat respectfully, graciously around the table, and
monkeys did tricks, and musical birds trilled at their master's
command, and at the same time — a marvel described by Marco
Polo and Oderic of Pordenone — the cups of wine flew to the
table like doves, from the hands of the chief server at the
banquet table, without a drop of the beverage being spilled — and
they were golden cups, of course. Golden, because everything
was made of gold in that marvelous country I sought, with the
sinking sensation that with each day's run I was farther away
from it. Perhaps, if we had sailed farther south from Cuba; or
perhaps, if we had gone north from Isabella . . . And now those
shit-assed Indians did nothing but confuse me: the ones from
Hispaniola, perhaps to get me off the track of their gold mines,
kept telling me to keep going — it's up ahead, farther but not too
far, "you're getting warmer, warmer, warmer," as if we were
playing find-the-button, you're nearly there — urging me to
keep on sailing; the Indians we had captured, on the other hand,
probably because they were afraid I would take them even
farther from their little island homes, told me that if I followed
that advice I would wind up in a country populated by cannibals
with a single eye in the head of a dog — monsters that sustained
themselves on nothing but the flesh and blood of humans. And
with all this I still hadn't found the immense treasure I was
seeking. For while Hispaniola seemed to hold more gold than
Cuba, to judge from the jewelry of the caciques and from the

little nuggets they gave us, and so must have been the location of the vein of gold, the Mother Lode, the mine, the huge mine — which had been mentioned time and again by the Venetians — I could find no trace of it anywhere. And this mine, this huge and wonderful mine, became an obsession with me . . . Now, with death hovering over me, as I await the confessor who is so slow to arrive, I reexamine the yellowed pages, with their faint, lingering smell of saltpeter, of the rough draft of the Account of My First Voyage, and I am horrified, filled with shame and sorrow, to see how many times the word GOLD appears there. Especially since, to prepare for my death, I have assumed the robes of a minor order of Franciscans, who are poor because they choose poverty, they wish to be poor, to be wed, as was Saint Francis of Assisi, to Our Lady of the Poor . . . It's as if witchcraft, an infernal vapor, had tarnished this manuscript so that it seems more a search for the Land of the Golden Calf than for the Promised Land, to ransom the millions of souls sunk in the vile shadows of idolatry. It made me angry at myself to see, for example, that on the twenty-fourth of December, when I should have been meditating, as a Franciscan, on the divine event of the Nativity, I wrote the word GOLD five times in ten lines that could have been taken from the grimory of an alchemist. Two days later, on the Feast of Saint Stephen, instead of thinking of the blessed death — by rocks and stones more precious than any gold — of the first martyr of the religion whose cross was displayed on our sails, I wrote the word GOLD a dozen times in an account in which I mentioned the Lord God only once — and that time only as part of a secular expression. And it is in just such thoughtless expressions as those that I used the name of the All-Powerful fourteen times in a general account in which GOLD is mentioned more than two hundred. And "Our Lord" is even used — I recognize this now with horror — almost as a polite formula accompanying the words *Your Highnesses* in talk intended to flatter, or it is used as a sort of propitiatory incantation—"Thanks be to God," "Through the grace of God"—when, with a false piety that stinks of brimstone, of the cloven-hoofed devil, I keep myself from saying *Our Lord should have showed me where the GOLD was*. Not only that, but on just one occasion—the twelfth of December—was the name of Jesus Christ finally inscribed in my text. Except for that one day, that exceptional occasion when I remembered I was a Christian, I invoked *God* and *Our Lord* in a way that revealed how much more profoundly my mind had been shaped by the Old Testament than by the Gospels, how much closer I felt to the God of Wrath with his furies and favors than to the parable of the Good Samaritan, on this voyage where, to tell the truth, neither Matthew, Mark, Luke, nor John was with us. We had left the Holy Books in Spain, they hadn't crossed the Ocean Sea, hadn't arrived in the new world, where no one intended to baptize anyone or save any of the souls whose ignorance sadly condemned them to die without understanding the meaning of the Cross made by our carpenters from planed and joined wood, and planted all up and down the coast as the Spanish claimed it. The Gospels, as I said, were left at home, rather than being launched in an attack, an army of sacred verses, against the religions I found here—although I was careful not to talk about them—revealed by the primitive sculptures, human figures, which I left where they were without much thought because they were only large stones . . . And here, in these papers, I have spoken only—with a single exception—of the *Lord* of Abraham and Jacob, the one who spoke to Moses from the burning bush—the *Lord* before his Incarnation, and I have absolutely ignored the Holy Spirit, who appears in my account less often than Mohammed . . . Realizing that now, as the soft sound of rain drowns out the steps of the droves of beasts that carry oil and vinegar in my street, realizing that, I tremble with fear . . . I turn the pages of my journal, searching, searching, searching. But no, no, no. The Incarnation was not entirely forgotten in

these pages because, after I named the first island I discovered —
on the fifteenth of October — for Saint Mary of the Divine
Conception, after I celebrated the feast day of Saint Mary of O —
on the eighteenth of December — by shooting off our Lombardy
guns, while we were on our way home, one day — the fourteenth
of February — made me recognize the Divine Power of the
Virgin, universally venerated by Christian sailors. I am over-
whelmed by my memory of that night, when the wind swelled
and the waves were terrifying, crashing one against the other,
*breaking over the ship and so hindering it that it could neither move
forward nor escape them.* In the clamor of the storm, Martín
Alonso's caravel was separated from us — which, I confess, yes, I
should confess it, did not cause me any great grief at the time,
since for quite some time now the overweeningly proud captain
had been standing up against me, disobeying my orders with
such disrespect for my authority that, a little earlier, while we
were sailing along the coast of Hispaniola, he had gone off for
several days, looking for gold, according to his story, with the
help of several rogues from the rowdy and muttering mob that
was set against me by Juan de la Cosa and that other malicious
villain Vicente Yáñez . . . (Ah, the Spaniards, the Spaniards, the
Spaniards. . . I have been thoroughly fucked by their propensity
to split up, to splinter, to divide into groups, form factions, in
perennial discord! . . .) So, that night we were surrounded by
such a terrible tempest I thought the ships would be engulfed by
the sea, and I attributed this disaster — and here I say it — *to my
lack of faith and confidence in Divine Providence.* It was then — and
only then! — that I had recourse to the divine intercession of the
Virgin in whose belly, as Saint Augustine said, "God made a Son
in the shape of a Man." Then I cast my lot with those who
pledged pilgrimages, promising Saint Mary of Guadalupe that I
would bring her a Pascal candle made from five pounds of wax;
and I promised another one to Saint Mary of Loreto, who is in
the lighthouse at Ancona, near the Pope; to Saint Claire of

Moguer I promised I would keep an all-night vigil and have a
Mass said. And we all, each and every one of us, made a vow that
as soon as we reached land we would go in our undershirts, in
procession, to pray in a church where Our Lady is worshipped . . . That done, I wrote a very brief account of our
journey, intended for Their Highnesses, and threw it into the
sea in a barrel, in case our ships were wrecked. And to my
misery and disgust, in the middle of this terrifying storm,
several scoundrels accosted me to say that if we were going to
sink, it was because, with my pitiful knowledge of seafaring, I
had not loaded the ships with ballast as heavily as I should have,
not foreseeing that when we returned, the barrels that had been
full on the voyage out with beef and pickles and flour and wine,
long since eaten and drunk, would be empty. And as this last
was sadly true, I accepted the humiliation of admitting it as a
punishment for my lack of faith — wickedly pleased, nonethe-
less, and I couldn't help it, that the swine Martín Alonso had
been lost during the terrible night, that he couldn't testify
against me if we were spared from the dreadful fury of the
elements . . . (Martín Alonso, driven by the wind, landed on
the coast of Galicia, where he wrote the king and queen a letter
that was filled to the brim with infamies: but I was favored by
Divine Providence, which let me live to approach the Court,
though bent under the weight of his calumnies. May the soul of
that miserable little bastard be consumed in the flames of
hell! . . .) As for me — and it is another charge against my
conscience that weighs upon me in the hour of my final
accounting — I don't remember, no, I don't remember — but
perhaps it was obscured by my failing memory — having kept
the promise I made to Saint Mary of Guadalupe, since so many
cares and concerns, so many surprises deflected my steps, dis-
tracting me, when I arrived . . . And I think now that the many
afflictions I have suffered since that time stemmed from that
unpardonable omission.

nder a brilliant April sun, the peerless city of Seville welcomed me like a conquering prince returned from the grandest victory, with joy and jubilation, with banners and bells, with compliments showering down and tributes from the balconies, with the music of organs and the trumpets of heralds, the bustle of a Corpus Christi procession, and the noise of flutes and bagpipes and oboes. And after the rejoicing and the fiestas and the banquets and the balls, I received my greatest reward: a letter from Their Highnesses inviting me to court, which was in Barcelona at this time of year, and—even more important to me—directing me to start immediately to organize a new voyage to the lands I had discovered. Caesar entering Rome in a triumphal chariot could not have felt more proud than I! Reading between the lines of the letter, I thought I saw the satisfaction and praise of one who considered my achievement, in some sense, as a token of victory placed at the feet of his Lady by a knight, a hero like those whose deeds are celebrated in romances . . . Impatient to see her again, it didn't take any more than that for me to start off, with my boxes of trophies, those parrots that were still alive—a bit runny-nosed and lackluster after their long trip, I had to admit—and, especially, my little band of Indians. Though I must say that those Indians, their eyes full of hate, were the only cloud—black cloud—casting a dark shadow on the vast horizon stretching toward the west that had just been opened up for me again, and much more safely this time. For of the ten captives we had taken, three were at death's door, and the physics that cure us—clysters, sweet drinks, suppositories, and leeches—do not help these men, who are prostrated by a cold, in agony, the life departing from them in fevers and shakes. For these three, it was quite obviously too late for the apothecary; it was that morbid hour when one must fetch the carpenter. As for the others, they seemed to be heading in the same direction, although their faces still brightened a little when I brought them a good jug of wine—something I was careful to do both morning and night. And the problem isn't that they drink constantly to get drunk—which helps them bear the inevitable pain they feel because of their exile from their country—rather it's that feeding them creates a difficult problem. To start with, they consider milk from a goat or a cow to be the most disgusting beverage any man could taste, they are amazed that we swallow this animal fluid, good only for nursing the beasts that fill them with misgivings and even fear, because before we came they had never seen these beasts with horns and udders, which are not found on their islands. Dried beef and salt fish repel them. They find our fruits repugnant. They spit out cabbage and turnips, and even the most succulent stews, claiming they're inedible. They like only garbanzo beans, because they taste a little, but only a little—according to Diegito, the only one we have managed to teach a few words of Spanish— like a food from their country, *maize,* a few sacks of which I have carried along, but which I've always scorned, not considering it fit for civilized people, though it might, perhaps, be good enough for pigs and asses. For all that, I think wine, although they have grown all too fond of it, can sustain them through their stubborn fast and give them strength for the new journey that was now planned. But that still left the question of the clothes for their presentation to the sovereigns. Out of respect for Their Majesties, they couldn't appear in court almost naked, the way they did in their own nation. And if they dressed the way we did, they wouldn't look that different from certain Andalusians with tan complexions—or from Christians mixed with Moors, of which we have a few in Spain. Luckily, at this critical moment, I was visited by a Jewish tailor I had met the year before near the Puerta de la Judería in Lisbon, where he had a shop, and who now, having gone from circumcised to Genoan—like so many others!—found himself in the city. He advised me to put them in red breeches sewed with little gold threads ("That's it . . . Perfect!" I said), loose shirts that expose their chests, which are smooth and hairless, and, on their heads, headpieces like tiaras, also of gold thread ("That's it . . . Perfect!" I repeated, "as good as gold"), filled with exquisite feathers—although not from the birds on their islands—that drape gracefully down the backs of their heads, over their black manes, which grew quite a bit during our voyage, and which I would now have to wash and curry like the coat of a horse, on the morning of the day of the presentation.

And the day arrived. All Barcelona was celebrating. Like a trader who enters a castle with a magnificent exhibition, I entered the palace where she awaited me, followed by the fabulous company that would perform the Spectacle of the Marvels of the Indies—first spectacle of its kind ever presented in the great theater of the universe—a company that I left in the bedroom, in an order determined several days before when I directed the rehearsals and arranged the characters. Escorted by heralds and ushers, I entered Their Majesties' throne room, slowly, solemnly, with the tread of a conqueror, without losing my poise or being dazzled by the splendor of the ceremony or the applause that greeted me—particularly pleasing was the sound of the applause of the many who were now repenting ever having been my enemy. My compass and beacon, on this walk down the crimson carpet that led straight to the royal platform, was the face of my sovereign, illuminated at this moment by the most ineffable smile. After I kissed the royal hands, she bade me take a seat—me, the renowned Genoan, the Genoan with hidden roots and an ancestry that I alone knew—between Castile and Aragon; the grand entrance door opened again and, walking two by two, carrying them on high, the porters brought in my trophies. On large silver trays—very large to make my display seem more impressive—the GOLD: chunks of gold, almost as large as a man's hand; delicate gold masks; gold figurines, devoted, no doubt, to some idolatry that for now I was very careful to keep quiet; little beads of gold; nuggets of gold; tiny plates of gold—not as much gold, to tell the truth, as I had hoped: gold that suddenly seemed too little gold, much too little gold, next to the jewels, the coats of arms, the embroidery that whirled around me, the gold tapestries, gold maces held by bearers, the gold borders of the canopy—too little gold, when all was said and done. Just the first glint of gold, behind which, far off in the distance, one can glimpse more gold, and more gold, and more gold . . . But now the Indians were entering—summoned by the captain who blew the lion-tamer's whistle that was used to tell them to do this or that—and on their hands and arms and shoulders they carried all the parrots that were still alive, more than twenty—all tremendously agitated by the movement and voices of those present for this occasion; besides, before the procession of marvels from across the sea made its entrance, I had given them many crumbs soaked in red wine, which made them raise such a hubbub that I was afraid they would suddenly start talking, repeating the bad words they had certainly heard on board the ship and during their stay in Seville. And after the Indians knelt down in front of Their Majesties, howling and sobbing, palsied, frenzied (begging the sovereigns to free them from the captivity in which I had enchained them, to return them to their homelands, although I explained that they were thrilled, trembling with joy, at being prostrate before the Spanish throne . . .), some of my sailors came in, carrying the skins of snakes and lizards, larger than any found here, and branches, dried leaves, and withered vegetation, which we displayed as examples of valuable spices, although nobody was really looking at them, all eyes were fixed

on the prostrate Indians—who were still sobbing and howling—and on the green parrots who had started to vomit cheap
red wine all over the royalties' red carpet. Seeing that the
spectacle was starting to get out of control, I sent the Indians out
with their birds, and the sailors with their plants, and I got to my
feet, facing Their Majesties, and showing my profile to the
brilliant assembly that filled the room—which, I have to admit,
was suffocatingly warm, and full of the sour smell of sweat-
soaked silk, satin, and velvet—and I began to speak. I spoke
slowly at first, describing the drama of the voyage, our arrival in
the Indies, our encounter with its inhabitants. To describe these
new lands, I evoked the beauty of Spain's most celebrated
regions, the sweetness—I knew what I was doing—of the fields
of Córdoba, although I certainly moderated my tone when I
compared the mountains of Hispaniola with the summits of
Teide. I told of seeing three sirens, on the ninth day of January,
in a place where there were numerous tortoises—ugly sirens, to
tell the truth, and with the faces of men, not the beautiful,
musical temptresses I had seen, like Ulysses (what a whopper!)
off the coasts of Malagueta. Since it's easy to keep on talking
once you get started, I gradually became inspired by my own
words, enlarging my gestures, stepping back to allow my voice
to resound, listening to myself as I would to somebody else, and
the names of the most splendid lands, both real and fabled,
began to roll off my tongue. Every gleaming, glistening, glittering, dizzying, dazzling, exciting, inviting image in the hallucina-
tory vision of a prophet came unbidden to my mouth as if
impelled by a diabolical interior energy. Without my willing it,
Hispaniola was transfigured by this inner music, so that it no
longer resembled Castile and Andalusia, oh no! it grew, it
swelled, until it achieved the fabulous heights of Tarsus, of
Ophir or Ophar, and finally reached the borders, which I had
found at last—yes, found!—of the fabulous kingdom of
Cipango. And there, in that very place, was the incredibly rich

mine mentioned by Marco Polo, and I had come to announce the fact to this kingdom and to all of Christendom. Colchis, Land of Gold, had been found, not in a pagan myth this time, but in its consummate reality. And gold was noble, and gold was good: *Genoans, Venetians, anyone who has pearls, precious stones, anything of great value, they all are willing to travel to the ends of the world to trade, to exchange these things for gold; gold, the greatest good; gold, the greatest treasure; whoever has gold can have anything in the world and can even attain paradise* . . . And with this voyage of mine, this amazing voyage of mine, the prophecy of Seneca has been fulfilled. Now . . .

Venient annis
saecula seris quibus Oceanus
uincula rerum laxet . . .

Here I cut the verse short, because I had the disconcerting impression — perhaps I was mistaken — that Columba, giving me an almost imperceptible wink, was looking at me with an expression that said: *Quosque tandem, Christoforo?* . . . All the same, making my voice more dramatic, I moved to a higher register: And, through the grace of Your Majesties, I was the one who opened, I was the one who led the way to new horizons, making the world round, like a pear, like the breast of a woman with a nipple in the middle — and my eyes quickly sought those of my Mistress — the world that Pedro Aliaco, the illustrious chancellor of the Sorbonne and Notre Dame de Paris, had seen as *almost* round, *almost* spherical, creating a bridge between Aristotle and me. With me, the prophesy in the Book of Isaiah is fulfilled. Now it has achieved reality: "Their land is filled with silver and gold, and there is no end to their treasures, in a place of broad rivers and streams, where galleys with oars can go, and stately ships can pass."

When I had finished, I knelt down for vespers with a studied expression of nobility, the monarchs knelt down, all those

present knelt down, choking back tears, as the six canons and
subcanons of the Royal Chapel began the most solemn *Te Deum*
ever heard this side of heaven. And when the celestial voices
came back to earth, I ordered my seven Indians to begin instruction in Christianity, so that they could be baptized as soon as
they had received enough knowledge. "Do not keep them as
slaves," said the Queen, "but take them back to their land in the
first ship returning there . . ." And that night, I came to see my
mistress in the intimacy of her private suite, where I knew the
pleasures of seeing her again after a long and difficult absence —
and damned if, during those hours, I remembered either caravels or Indians. But a little before sunrise, when we were both
lying sated, watching the sky begin to brighten, talking of one
thing and another, I thought I noticed that Columba, having had
time to reconsider the events of the day and recognize the
realities I knew so well, did not seem as completely convinced
by my words as I might have wished. I increased my rhetoric,
the aptness of my quotations, the skill with which I manipulated
images, but she was reserved, reticent, she wouldn't commit
herself or express a frank and full opinion about the importance
of my enterprise. "So, in a word . . . what do you think of what
you saw today?" I asked, to get her started. "What I think is, to
bring back seven bleary-eyed little men, sick and sorrowful, a
few sticks and leaves that aren't good for anything but fumigat-
ing a leper colony, and gold that wouldn't fill a cavity in a molar,
it's not worth having spent two million maravedis." "And what
about the value to your crowns?" I shouted. "We gained enough
prestige with the expulsion of the Jews and the conquest of the
kingdom of Granada. Real, lasting prestige comes from things
that can be seen and touched, from laws that have repercussions
as far away as Rome, from military victories that become part of
history . . . But your prestige, if in fact you earn any, will be in
the long term. Up to this point, nothing has happened in these
countries, which we can't even imagine, no battles have been

won, no memorable triumphs have been achieved — *in hoc signo vinces* — for now, all we have is inspiration that makes blind men cheer and opinions that make your listeners swell up with pleasure, like the heroic feats Charlemagne recounted when he made his victorious entrance to Zaragoza, having humiliated the Babylonian king, when the truth was that, after a siege that was neither glorious nor arduous, he returned to France defeated, leaving a rear guard commanded by Roland the knight, who ... well! ... you know what happened ..." "But I brought back gold!" I insisted: "Everybody saw it. There is a mine there, an enormous mine ..." "If the mine is so big, your men should have brought back ingots, not the trifles that my jewellers say are not even worth a hundred maravedis." I said it was impossible, in the short time we were *over there*, to undertake the real job of extraction; of the importance of returning as soon as possible to tell of my Discovery ... "I had an expert in aromatic plants identify the plants you brought back: he didn't find any cinnamon, or any nutmeg, or pepper, or cloves: therefore, you did not land in the Indies," she said. "Always the imposter." "Then where did I land?" "In a place nothing like any part of the Indies." "And in so doing, I risked my honor and my life." "Not really. Not really. If you hadn't met Master Jacob in Ice Land, you wouldn't have gone off so confidently. You knew that, *no matter what*, come what may, you would arrive at some country." "A country that holds fabulous treasures!" "Apparently not, from what you have shown us." "Then why in the devil did you write to me, ordering me to prepare for a second voyage?" "To screw Portugal," she answered, calmly biting off a piece of Toledan marzipan. "If we don't establish a firm foothold now, the others will get in ahead of us — the ones to whom you almost sold your project, twice, the rulers of Castile and Aragón matter so little to you. They've already sent messengers to the Pope, claiming possession of the lands that your ships barely touched." "So my voyage didn't accomplish anything?" "I wouldn't go that far. But, hell! . . . how complicated life is! Now I have to outfit ships, raise money, postpone the war in Africa, all in order to plant our flag—I have no choice—in countries that, as far as I'm concerned, are neither Ophir, Ophar, nor Cipango. Try to bring back more gold than you brought this time, and pearls, and precious stones, and spices. Then I'll believe in some of these things that still smell to me like more of your tricks." . . . When I left the royal bedchamber, I was really stung, I must confess. Some of the things she said made my ears burn. But I was not as upset as I had been before, when no one would finance my proposals. Once again the ocean was in sight. Within a few months, I would again feel the excitement of billowing sails, but with a luff more full and secure than before . . . And now I would have enough ships; now that scoundrel Martín Alonso was dead; now I would really command my crew, with the title of Admiral, my appointment as Viceroy, and the *Don* in front of my name . . . I returned to the dockyard where the Indians were shivering under their wool coverlets, and the parrots, having finished vomiting the wine they had gulped down, were lying with their feet in the air, with the glassy eyes of dead fish gone bad, droopy, their feathers ruffled, as if they had been chased by a broom . . . Soon they would all be dead. As would six of the seven Indians I had exhibited before the throne—some dying of a cough, some of measles, some of diarrhea—a few days after being baptized. From Diegito, the only one left, I knew that these men neither liked nor admired us: they thought we were treacherous, lying, violent, hot-tempered, cruel, dirty, and foul-smelling, since we almost never bathed, unlike them, who freshened their bodies several times a day in the rivers, streams, and waterfalls of their land. They said our houses stank of rancid grease; our narrow streets of shit; our finest horsemen of armpits; and that if our ladies wore so many bodices and ruffles and ribbons, it must be to hide some repulsive deformity or sore—or maybe because they're embarrassed by their breasts, which are so fat that they always seem ready to pop out of their lace tuckers. Our perfumes and scented oils — and even incense — make them sneeze; they choke in our narrow rooms; and they think our churches are places of pain and panic because of the many filthy, crippled, pathetic dwarfs and monsters who clog their entrances. They can't understand why so many men who are not part of an army go about armed, nor how so many richly dressed women on dazzling horses can look down without shame on the perpetual grieving demonstration of misery and purulence, of amputees and beggars in rags. Not only that, but our plan to inculcate in them the doctrines of our religion, before they would receive the lustral waters, had come to nothing. They didn't say that they were unwilling to listen: they said, simply, that they did not understand. If God had created the world and the plants and the animals that populate it, and had pronounced everything in it to be good, they could not see how Adam and Eve, creatures of Divine Creation, could have committed any offense by eating the good fruit from the good tree. They did not think that going perfectly naked was indecent: if the men *over there* wore a loincloth it was because their fragile, sensitive sex, hanging exposed, had to be protected from spiny plants, sharp grasses, and from the attacks, blows, and cuts of predators; as for the women, it was better that they cover their nature with the little pieces of cotton I had seen, so that when the menses was flowing, that distasteful pollution would not be obvious. They did not understand the Old Testament books I showed them either: they could not see why evil was represented by a serpent, since the serpents in their islands were not dangerous. Moreover, the idea of a serpent with an apple in his mouth made them laugh uproariously because — as Diegito explained to me — "snakes don't eat fruit" . . . Soon we will raise anchor once again and return to the outposts of Cipango that I discovered — although Columba, who was insufferable during this period, perhaps because she needed an outlet for her anxiety, said a hundred times that she had seen no sign of Cipango. And as for the indoctrination of the Indians, she should have employed men more capable than I to perform that mission! Saving souls is not my job. And don't look for the vocation of an apostle in someone who has the gall of a banker. And now what she asked me to do — it was more an order — was to find gold, lots of gold, as much gold as I could, since now — thanks to me — a mirage had been created, a vision of Colchis and the Golden Chersonese.

slands, islands, islands . . . A large one, a tiny one, a harsh one, a mild one; a bald island, a hairy island, an island with gray sand and dead lichens; an island with pebbles churned up, submerged, buried to the rhythm of each successive wave; a broken-up island—with a saw-toothed shoreline; a swollen island—as if pregnant, the pyramidal shape of a dormant volcano; an island within an arc of fish and parrots; an island with austere points, sharp snail shells, mangrove thickets with a thousand hooks; an island surrounded by foam, like a little girl in a lace skirt; an island with the music of castanets and an island with roaring gorges; an island to run aground on, an island to be stranded on, an island with neither name nor history; an island where the wind sings through the cavities of enormous shells; an island with coral-like water flowers; an island with an inactive volcano; a moss-green island, a chalk-gray island, a salt-white island; islands in such a tight and sunny constellation—I have counted a hundred and four—that, thinking what to call them, I have named them *Gardens of the Queen* . . . Islands, islands, islands. More than five thousand islands, the Venetian chronicles tell us, surround the great kingdom of Cipango. So I must be approaching that great kingdom . . . And yet, as the days go by, I see the color of gold receding from me, because, while the mineral keeps appearing, here, there, in the form of jewelry, figurines, beads, little bits—which are hardly ever even the size of a good Genoan hand—all of these are merely flecks, light traces, the barest hints of a great vein that has not yet appeared—and which was not found in Hispaniola, after all, as I had expected when I was under the illusion that it was an island of great riches. And

109

now in my account of my second voyage, I begin to feel the need
to make excuses. I send word to Their Highnesses that I would
have liked to have sent them a great quantity of gold, but I can't,
because my men have been stricken by so many diseases. I claim
that what I have sent should be regarded only as *signs*. Because
there is more: there is surely much more. And so I go on,
searching, hoping, anxious, avid, and always more disillusioned,
unable to find the source mine, the Mother Lode, the great bed,
the supreme asset of these lands of spices without any
spices . . . Now, in this house where it seems to be getting dark
before it should, waiting for the confessor who should have
been here by now, considering the closeness of the miserable
little village where they've gone to look for him, I keep turning
the pages of the drafts of my journals and letters. And viewing
myself through words I wrote years ago, I observe, looking
backward, that a diabolical change was taking place in my soul.
Angered by those Indians who did not divulge their secret to
me, who now hid their women when we arrived at their villages
because there were among us some lewd and lascivious men;
vexed by those mistrustful and insolent people who still, from
time to time, shot arrows at us — although without doing us
much harm, to tell the truth — I stopped seeing them as kind,
gentle, innocent beings, as incapable of malice as they were of
seeing their nudity as shameful, which is the idyll I had painted
for my sponsors when I returned from my first voyage. Now,
more and more often, I call them *cannibals* — although I had
never seen them eating human flesh. The India of spices has
become for me the *India of Cannibals*. Not very dangerous
cannibals — I insist — but cannibals who must not remain ignorant of our holy religion; cannibals whose souls must be saved
(suddenly this becomes my obsession!), as millions of men and
women in the pagan world were saved by the word of the
Apostles of the Lord. But, since there is obviously no way of
indoctrinating these cannibals, because we do not speak their

languages, which I am discovering are many and distinct, the solution to this grave problem, which cannot be indifferent to the Church, is to take them to Spain as slaves. I have said: *as slaves.* Yes, now that I am at the gates of death the word appalls me, but in the account that I reread it is clearly written in my large, round hand. I requested a license for the *slave trade.* I maintained that the cannibals of these islands would be *better than any other slaves,* arguing, at the same time, that they can live on anything and that they eat much less than the blacks that are so numerous in Lisbon and Seville. (Since I cannot deliver gold, I think, I can substitute the irreplaceable energy of human flesh, a work force whose value lies in what it produces, which, in the final analysis, is of greater value than a mineral that comes in one hand and goes out the other . . .) Moreover, to prove my point, I sent several of those cannibals—whom I selected as the most able-bodied—along with *women, boys, and girls,* by ship to see how they would grow and reproduce in Spain, as had been done with the captives imported from Guinea. And I explained that with royal permission we could send caravels every year to obtain good shiploads of cannibals, whom we could deliver punctually in any quantity desired, hunting down the populations of the islands and keeping them in fenced camps until it was time to embark. And if it was objected that we lacked the manpower for such a task, I implored them to let me have some thousand men and a few hundred horses, so that I could begin tilling the earth and establishing wheat and grapes and grazing cattle. The people would have to be paid wages against the island's yields, but it was my thought—an ingenious plan of which I was disgracefully proud at the time—that they would not have to be paid in money: some stores would be set up in the royal hacienda to provide clothes, cheap shirts and jackets, handkerchiefs, coats, trousers, and shoes, as well as medicines, cures, and miscellaneous pharmaceuticals, *surplus* goods and Spanish products that *the people here would accept gratefully to alleviate their misery.* (In short, they would be paid in our goods, which would be a profitable arrangement, since they would never see a penny, and, anyway, money would do them little good, they would quickly incur lifelong debts, signing for their purchases . . .) Considering, however, that the roundup of slaves that I proposed would be sure to meet with some resistance on the part of the cannibals, I requested — a prepared man is as good as two — the shipment of *two hundred cuirasses, one hundred muskets, and a hundred crossbows,* along with the materials necessary to maintain and repair them . . . And I concluded my catalog of shameful proposals, written in Isabella City on the thirtieth of January, 1496, by begging God to give me *one good deposit of gold* — as if I had not fallen, on that day, into His disfavor, by initiating the slave trade. (Instead of begging His pardon and doing penance, miserable one, I asked him for *one good deposit of gold,* the way a whore asks each day, facing the uncertain and long night ahead of her, to be favored by the providential apparition of a splendid and careless person with a free hand and a heavy purse! . . .)

ut when I wrote to Their Highnesses I was lying yet again, withholding propositions that, though they had matured in my mind (which is why I sent as advance evidence a number of captives with their women, sons, and daughters), I had actually kept back, for my return—when I would have an opportunity to advance or retract them, according to the reaction of my audience. But events had developed in so unfortunate a fashion that I found that others had followed the same line of thought, making an accomplished fact—a bloody reality—of what I had coolly conceived, waiting for the royal consent to initiate an action that would erase the memory of the many failures of my enterprise. And with pen flying I made a desperate effort to stem the tempest that, having cast me onto this island, could just as well fly back across the ocean and demolish the statue that I had managed through my labors to erect—although as yet unfinished and still somewhat shaky on its pedestal—on the Great Stage of Barcelona. What happened was that on my return from a discovery of nearby islands I had found the Spaniards changed, mindless of all authority, given to cruel projects dictated by their greed. They were all obsessed with gold, possessed by Gold Fever. But if their fever was like mine—since in blindly, cruelly seeking gold they were merely following my example—the causes of their frenzy were different from mine. I didn't want the gold for myself (at least, not yet . . .). I first needed to maintain my prestige with the court and to justify the legitimacy of the lofty titles that had been granted to me. I couldn't allow them to go on saying that my extremely costly enterprise had not yielded to the crown "enough gold to fill a tooth." My disease was that of a Grand Admiral. The sickness of those shit-assed Spaniards, by contrast, was that of scoundrels who wanted the mineral for themselves — to keep it, amass it, hide it, and leave these lands as soon as possible, their fortunes made, to indulge *back there* their particular vices, lusts, and appetites. In my absence, forgetting my instructions and ignoring my brother Bartholomew, whom, like me, they regarded as a foreigner, they had begun scouring all of Hispaniola for gold, beating the Indians, burning their villages, maiming, killing, torturing, in an effort to learn where, where, where, was the accursed invisible mine that I likewise sought — not to mention violating hundreds of women and girls in all their expeditions. Now the resistance of the natives was becoming organized to such a dangerous degree — though they could not match us in arms, they had a better command of the terrain — that I was forced to send troops into the interior. In a place that is still called La Vega Real the Spaniards took more than five hundred captives and imprisoned them nearby in a prison fortress with embrasures from which to fire at rebels — and I had no idea what to do with them. They could not be released, because they would carry the spirit of rebellion to other tribes. We didn't have sufficient provisions to feed them. To execute them all — as some urged me to do — seemed to me an excessive step, which might perhaps earn the censure of those who had granted me my titles — and I knew full well Columba's violent rages. But, faced with the accomplished fact, I had to rid myself — I had no alternative — of those five hundred prisoners who in an unlucky hour had been thrust upon me, so I decided — with my brother's agreement — to exploit the now irreversible situation, smoothing over, embellishing, justifying something that was nothing other than the perpetration of slavery in these lands. I demonstrated the many benefits of this institution, and even found my justification in the Gospels. And with the Gospels before the wind — the slave trade not yet having been authorized by the king — I placed the

Indians in two ships, lashed, kicked, and cudgeled, for want of any other solution to the conflict of authority in which I found myself. Moreover — a new trick — those slaves were not actually slaves (like the ones we obtained from Africa) but rebels against the Royal Crown, prisoners, unhappy but inevitable victims of a new *just and necessary war* [sic]. Carried to Spain, they ceased to be dangerous. And each one became *a soul* — a soul that according to the mandate of I-know-not-which Gospel, is rescued from certain idolatry, which is devil worship, like all the idolatries I had begun to rail against more and more in my letters and journals, arguing that certain decorative masks on the headbands of the caciques represented the silhouette of Beelzebub. (So, since the first step is the one that counts the most, Bartholomew soon received instructions from me to fill three more ships with that human booty that, for the moment, would replace the gold that did not appear anywhere . . .)

. . . And in the dawn of our second homecoming, amid the boisterous bustle of the sailors' disembarking, with its guaranteed delights of wild dances, strong wine, and whores for all, I was bedecked with my best Grand Admiral's court dress, when my joy was redoubled by the sight of Master Jacob, who, after embracing me, told me that he was passing through here to pick up a big load of Andalusian wine for the Irish of Saint Patrick — they were growing greater drunkards every day. "I hear you've been to Vinland," he said, reaching for the wineskin that, to fortify myself, I had half emptied. "Vinland is good," I said, without confirming or denying his statement, "but farther south there are lands that are better still." And once more I embraced him, because I was delighted to see him again, after so many tribulations, believing his unexpected presence to be an augur of good fortune — I was, I repeat, delighted, when my delight was choked as if by a sponge soaked in vinegar on learning that, after having made in Seville an advantageous sale of a number of my Indians captured in Hispaniola, there had arrived, harsh and fulminating, a royal order prohibiting the flourishing trade that I had advised and set up. It seemed that Their Highnesses, attacked by scruples, had convened a commission of theologians and canons to determine if such commerce was licit, and those who had always been my enemies had pronounced, as always, against my interests. Thus the sales of more than two hundred slaves were nullified and two days' profits had to be returned. Those who had already taken their Indians with the promise of quick payment had to return the human merchandise, remaining free of debt. And henceforth I was severely prohibited from shipping new captives to Spain, which meant that I would have to close my internment camps on the islands, suspending the capture of men and women—the task so magnificently begun. I began to cry, from sheer outrage, on Master Jacob's shoulder. They have shut down the one fruitful trade that, in compensation for the lack of gold and spices, I had discovered! On this second return, which I had pictured as full of glory, I saw myself ruined, discredited, disempowered, disapproved by Their Highnesses and even called a *fraud* [sic] by the same people who had acclaimed me the day before! And the sailors were still waiting for me to descend from the ships for their wonderful, triumphal landing! . . . How miserable, lamentable, ridiculous my brilliant suit seemed to me then, my breeches, cap of golden cloth, the insignia of a Grand Admiral! . . . And then there appeared in me, as often before, the goliard who hid under my skin, when, for want of better recourse, I put on a grim, doleful mask, like the mask of a martyr in a sacred picture. I changed quickly. I quickly assumed the habit of the lower Franciscan order, with cord belt, bare feet, and shaved head. And with my eyes clouded with a great show of sadness, contrite and almost in tears, back bent, shoulders slumped, I signaled, with all the show of submission of a penitent in Holy Week, to the first of my incredulous sailors to disembark. *Kyrie eleison* . . . But, in the first line of those who pressed forward to join me in my return to shore I saw the face, wry, ironic, and condemning, of that Rodrigo de Triana whose ten thousand reales of royal reward I had taken to give to Beatriz, my spurned lover. I detected in his look a note of accusation, and I also observed that the sailor still carried, as a sign of his contempt, the silk doublet that I had given him *that day* — now worn and mended all over, but still with its ostentatious red color, the color of the devil. And, alarmed, I asked myself whether the presence of Rodrigo, here, today, was not the presence of the one lying in wait to try to drag me to the Kingdom of Shadows, whether at that moment he was beginning his effort to call me to account. I had made no pact with him. But there are pacts not made on paper, not signed in blood. They remain written, in indelible ink, when with lies and deceits, inspired by the Malignant One, we enjoy wonders denied to other mortals. In spite of the Franciscan habit in which I now enveloped myself, my flesh was like that of the Pseudo-Cyprian, the Cartagenian heretic who pledged his soul to regain his lost youth and shamefully take advantage of the innocence of a maiden — a virgin as pure and innocent of the Evil of Gold as were the lands that I had opened to the greed and lust of men from here: *Kyrie eleison.*

nother trip and then another, remembered here, on the verge of leaving on the journey from which there will be no return, on this sad Valladolid dusk when I am faintly illuminated by two candles brought by a servant of velvet step who passes by me without asking any questions, seeing me deep in the anguished reading of old papers, turned over on the sheet—already practically a shroud—of this bed where my enfeebled elbows stretch the serge of the minor habit of my order, with which, perhaps without deserving it, I have chosen to wrap my wasted body . . . Another trip and another trip, and still I had not found the *one good deposit of gold*—such money-changer's language, the language of a Lombard banker!—sacrilegiously beseeching the Lord before whom I had taken a vow of poverty in token obeisance to a rule already widely abused in this century, to be honest—a part of a ceremony to which I had submitted myself in deference to the wishes of my Mistress. Not a good mass of gold, nor a good mass of pearls, nor a good mass of spices, nor a good mass obtained, otherwise, in the slave trade in Seville. And so, having tried to substitute the flesh of the Indies for the gold of the Indies, seeing that I could obtain neither gold nor flesh to sell, I began—apprentice of a prodigious magician—to substitute, for gold and flesh, words. Great, beautiful, weighty, juicy, rich words, raised in the brilliant court of wise men, doctors, prophets, and philosophers. Not having found the mine that Their Highnesses considered so important and longed for so intensely, I used magic to make them see that not all that shines is gold. The Crown of Portugal had amassed immense sums in prestigious navigations—without further material benefit—that spread its fame throughout the world. I knew that my

voyage cost much and yielded little. But I invoked the millions—
possibly millions—of souls that would be saved if they would
send good preachers *over there,* like those who accompanied Juan
de Monte Corvino in his diocese in Cambaluc. If I have not
"brought supplies of gold," much has been accomplished (and
this is not the least) *for the spiritual and the temporal.* And kings and
monarchs must inspire such enterprises, remembering that Solomon financed his ships in a three-year journey with the sole
object of seeing Mount Sopora; that Alexander dispatched emissaries to the island of Trapobana, in the other Indies, to obtain a
better knowledge of them; and that Nero Caesar (why did it
occur to me to cite that abominable persecutor of Christians?)
went to great pains to try to locate the source of the Nile. *These are
the things it has been given to princes to undertake.* And now . . . all
right! I have not found the Indies of the spices but the Indies of
the cannibals, but . . . shit! I had found nothing less than the
Earthly Paradise! Yes! Let the New Burnisher be known, be
heard, the name be spread in all the realms of Christianity! . . . The Earthly Paradise faces the island I have named
Trinidad, at the mouth of the Drago, where the fresh waters of
the heavens contend with the salt marshes—bitter with the many
sediments of the land. I saw it, precisely as it is, far from where
the deceived and deceiving cartographers had placed it, here,
there, its Adams and Eves moved—relocated—the tree between
them, the serpent tempter, the dwelling without fortifications,
domestic zoology, loving and chaste beasts, and all the rest,
according to the whim of each. I saw it. I saw what no one had
seen: the mountain in the shape of a woman's tit, or, more
precisely, of a nipple on a pear—oh, you, about whom are you
thinking?—establishing that the Garden of Genesis is *there* and
nowhere else, since many have spoken about it without manag-
ing to tell us where it is, because never have I found . . . *a
scripture in Greek or Latin that unequivocally locates the Earthly Paradise in this world, nor is it situated on any map of the world, except by the*

authority of argument. Some placed it at the source of the Nile in Ethiopia; others searched those lands and found no confirmation of it . . . *Saint Isadoro and Bede and Strabo and the scholastic master of history and Saint Ambrose and Scott and all the worthy theologians agree that the Earthly Paradise is in the Orient, etcetera* — is in the Orient, I repeat, not omitting the *etcetera,* because *etcetera* is something. So it must be placed in the Orient then, in an Orient which had to be an Orient because it was thought there existed only one possible Orient. But since I have reached the Orient by sailing west, I maintain that those who claimed this were mistaken, drawing fantastic maps, deceived by fables and fictions, because my eyes have seen the proof of what they could only imagine, that I have reached the one, true, authentic Earthly Paradise just as one would picture it based on the Holy Scriptures: a place where infinite varieties of trees grow, beautiful to look upon, whose fruits are delicious to the taste, where a great river flows whose waters mark the boundaries of *a region rich in gold* — and gold, I repeat and insist, lies there in enormous abundance, even though I have not been favored with the longed-for strike — the striver stricken for want of a strike . . . And, after invoking Isadoro, Ambrose, and Scott, true theologians, to screw the mediocre Spanish theologians of today who always oppose me, I resort to the science of Pliny, Aristotle, and, again, the vision of Seneca, to nestle in the incontrovertible authority of the ancients, endorsed — like Virgil, announcer of a New Age — by the Church itself . . . And, describing my fourth voyage, coasting alongside a land that shows no signs of being an island but rather terra firma — and very stable, with high mountains that hide unsuspected mysteries, possible cities, invaluable riches — I was possessed again by the spirit of greed, I found new energies, and immediately, facing the present reality, I realized that until then I had been rather hasty — not to say untruthful — in giving triumphant accounts: *When I discovered the Indies I said they were the greatest, richest dominion in the world. I spoke of gold, pearls, precious stones, stores, commerce, and fairs, and when it did not all appear immediately I was put to shame. This reproach makes me say now no more than* . . . *that I have seen in this land of Veragua more signs of gold in the two first days than in Hispaniola in four years, and that the lands of this territory could not be more beautiful nor more bountiful nor the people more faint-hearted* . . . *Your Highnesses are as much the lords of this land as of Jerez or Toledo; your ships that go there are going to your own home* . . . And what to do, now, with such riches? To fulfill, simply, the great aspiration of Christianity—what eight crusades had not achieved. What neither Peter the Hermit, nor Godefroy de Bouillon, nor Saint Bernard, nor Saint Louis of France had achieved would have to be obtained through the tenacity in the face of constant opposition of this son of a Savona tavern keeper. And, further, it is written: *Jerusalem and Mount Zion must be rebuilt by Christian hands,* and *The Abbot Joachim Calabrés said that this person would have to sally forth from Spain.* This person *would have to sally forth from Spain* —listen to that. He didn't say that he would have to be a Spaniard. And, speaking of myself, I could say like Moses in the land of Midian: "I am a stranger in a strange land." But these foreigners are the ones who find the Promised Lands. And therefore the one marked by a sign, the Chosen One, was I. Yet my path was long and difficult: *Seven years have I been in your Royal Court and everyone who heard of my enterprise said it was a mockery. Now even tailors apply for discovery.* And one day, the seventh of July, 1503, weak and miserable in the country of Jamaica, I thought that my constant boasting had raised me up too much in my own estimation, incurring the sin of pride; humble, finally, in a missive sent to my Kings, I said, *I did not undertake this voyage to earn honor or wealth; this is true, for all hope of that was already dead. I came to Your Highnesses with sincere intention and an honest zeal, and I did not lie* . . . I did not lie. I said that I did not lie. But when I look back at myself through the yellowed pages that lie upside down on the sheet drawn halfway up my chest . . .

hen I search through the labyrinth of my past, in this my final hour, I am astonished by my natural talents as an actor, as the life of the party, as a wielder of illusions, in the style of the mountebanks in Italy who, from fair to fair — and they came often to Savona — brought their comedies, pantomimes, and masquerades. I was an impresario of spectacles, taking my Pageant of Marvels from throne to throne. I was the promoter of a *sacred representation,* carrying out, for the Spaniards who came with me, the great act of the Taking Possession of Islands that did not even consent to be known. I was the magnificent organizer of the Great Landing in Barcelona — the first great spectacle of the West Indies, with authentic men and animals presented before the public of Europe. Later — it was during my third voyage — seeing that the Indians on one island appeared mistrustful, leery of approaching us, I improvised a scenario in the poop castle, making some Spaniards dance boisterously to the sound of the tambourine and the clapper, so that they would see that we were a merry people, pleasant in nature. (But it turned out badly for us on that occasion, to be honest, because the cannibals, not diverted by our Moorish dances and tapping heels, fired all the arrows they had in their canoes at us . . .) And, changing my colors, I was the Astrologer and Miracle Monger on that Jamaican beach where we found ourselves in the greatest misery, without food, diseased, and surrounded by countless hostile inhabitants, ready to launch an attack. Opportunely, it occurred to me to consult the *Efemerides* of Abraham Zacuto, which I always carried with me, in which I found that there would be an eclipse of the moon that February night, and I at once announced to our enemies that if they would hold their peace for a while longer, they would witness a great and astonishing sign. And, when the moment arrived, extending my arms like a windmill, gesticulating like a necromancer, reciting false spells, I ordered the moon to hide itself . . . and the moon hid itself. I returned at once to my cabin, and then waited for the hourglass to mark the time that the miracle would last—as was indicated in the text—and reappeared before the terrorized cannibals, ordering the moon to show itself again—which it did, without delay, attending my command. (Perhaps it was through such artifices that I have survived until today . . .) And I was the Grand Inquisitor, menacing and terrible—I don't want to recall that—that day when, on the shores of Cuba, I demanded of my mariners whether they had the least doubt that this great land was terra firma, the land of the continent, the outreaches of the vast Indies whose reward—slight reward!—awaited me in Spain. And I had proclaimed, through the voice of the notary, that anyone who argued with the judgment that the land of Cuba was a continent would pay a fine of ten thousand maravedis, and, moreover, would have his tongue cut out. *His tongue cut out.* No less. But the I-the-Inquisitor obtained what I was after. All the Spaniards—not forgetting the Galicians and Biscayans whom I always saw as a different people—swore and swore again, thinking in that way to preserve what, according to Aesop, is the best and the worst thing in the world. *I required that Cuba be a continent and a hundred voices rose to say that Cuba was a continent* . . . But the man who uses cheats, deceptions, threats, or violence to obtain a goal soon receives his punishment. And for me the punishment began here in this world, without waiting for the world beyond, since it was all misery, misfortune, and expiation of sins in my final voyage—a voyage in which I saw my ships surmounting waves like mountains and descending into roaring abysses, lifted, drenched, lashed, broken, before being carried again into the sea by a river of Veragua that was swollen with rain, suddenly, pushing us away, as if denying us asylum. And in those days of new calamities, after a last desperate search for gold on terra firma, we ended up in a misery of wrecked ships, itching sores, raging fevers, hunger, endless afflictions, when, almost passing out, I heard the voice of someone who said to me "Oh, foolish and slow in believing and serving your God, the God of all men!" wrenching me from the dark night of my desperation with words of courage, to which I responded with the promise of going to Rome, in a pilgrim's habit, if I could escape from so many tribulations with my life. (But my vow remained unfulfilled, like so many others I made . . .) And I returned to my point of departure, turned away, as they say, from the discovered world, remembering as nightmare creatures the *manikins of Cipango*—whom I mentioned in my testament yesterday—who, in the final analysis, never had any sense of having progressed to a better condition, regarding my appearance on their sands as a horrible misfortune. For them, Christophoros—a Christophoros who did not quote even a single verse of the Gospels in writing his letters and journals—was, in reality, the Prince of Calamities, Prince of Blood, Prince of Tears, Prince of Plagues—one of the horsemen of the Apocalypse. And as far as my conscience is concerned, to the image of me that arises now, as seen in a mirror, at the foot of this bed, I was the Discoverer discovered—discovered because *uncovered,* because my accounts and letters to my royal masters *uncovered* me; *uncovered* before God, on conceiving that foul commerce that, defying theology, I proposed to Their Highnesses; *uncovered* before my men whose respect I lost more every day, inflicting on me the supreme humiliation of a cook placing me in chains—me, Don, Admiral, and Viceroy!; *uncovered* because my route to the Indies or southern Vinland or Cipango or Cathay—whose province of Mangui could well be what I knew by the name of Cuba—the route I opened easily enough, knowing the sagas of the Normans, is a route used now by a hundred adventurers: even tailors, I said, having abandoned needle and thread for the oar; hidalgos without a penny, squires without a master, clerks without a position, coachmen without a team, soldiers without a commission, bald-faced picaros, swineherds from Cáceres, bullies in worn capes, slobs from Badajoz, intriguers blessed and patronized, awed by class, Christians whose names had been changed at the notary, baptized men who had only recently been to the baptismal font, rabble who did whatever they could to tear me down and wipe my name from the chronicles. Perhaps they no longer remember me, now that the fat is in the fire, now that they have gone beyond the boundaries of my expeditions, given name to cities—cities they call them!—of ten Indian huts covered with bird shit . . . I was the Discoverer-discovered, uncovered; and I am the Conquerer-conquered because I began to exist for me and for the others the day I reached *over there*, and since then, it is those lands that have formed me, sculpted my shape, defined me in the air that surrounds me, it is those lands that confer on me, in my own eyes, an epic stature that everyone denies me, especially now that Columba has died, bound to me in an exploit full of marvels worthy of a chivalric song—but a chivalric song erased, before being written, by the themes of the new romances that people want to hear now. Now they are saying that my enterprise was much less risky than the voyages of Vasco da Gama, who didn't hesitate to retake the route where several armadas had disappeared without a trace; less risky than that of the great Venetian who was missing for twenty-five years and given up for dead . . . And that is what the Spaniards say, who always view you as a foreigner. And that is because you have never had a homeland, mariner: that is why you had to search *over there*—in the West—where you are never defined in terms of national values, in days that were days when here it was night, in nights that were night when here it was day, rocking, like Absalom hanging by his hair, between dream and life, without ever learning where the dream began and the life ended. And now that you are entering the great dream that never ends, where unimaginable trumpets blare, you think that your only possible homeland—what perhaps will make you enter into legend, if a legend of yours is to be born—*is what as yet has no name,* what has acquired neither image nor word. *That which* as yet has not become an *Idea;* it has not acquired a conception, a defined outline, neither content nor what is contained. Any manikin from *over there* is more aware of *who one is,* in a land known and delimited, than you, mariner, with centuries of science and theology on your shoulders. Pursuing a country never found that fades away like a castle of enchantments each time you sing your victory song, you were a follower of vapors, seeing things that never became intelligible, comparable, explicable, in the language of the *Odyssey* or in the language of Genesis. You went into a world that played tricks on you when you thought you had conquered it and which, in reality, threw you off your course, leaving you with neither *here nor there.* Swimmer between two waters, shipwrecked between two worlds, today you will die, or tonight, or tomorrow, like a protagonist of fictions. Jonah vomited from the whale, sleeper of Ephesus, wandering Jew, captain of a ghost ship . . . But, in the final accounting without appeal or repeal, there is one thing that should never be forgotten: against the people who might have opposed you, you bore arms that had the advantage of thirty centuries of development, you bore the gift of unknown diseases; when you arrived in your vessels, you bore greed and lust, hunger for riches, the sword and the torch, the chain, the stocks, and the whip you had to crack in the dark night of the mines; you were the bearer of those things when you arrived like a man fallen from the sky—as you said to the rulers—dressed more in blue than in yellow, bearer, perhaps, of a successful mission. And remember, mariner, Isaiah, whom for so many years you had quoted to validate your always excessive words, your always unfulfilled promises: *Woe to those who are wise in their own eyes, and shrewd in their own sight!* And now remember Ecclesiastes, which you have read over so often: *He who loves gold is oppressed by the weight of his sin; he who pursued lucre will be the victim of lucre; inevitable was the ruin of he who was burdened with gold.* And, from deep within the thunder that now falls upon the wet roofs of the city, Isaiah's voice again calls to you, as you tremble with fright: *even though you make many prayers, I will not listen; your hands are full of blood* (I:15).

You hear, on the stairs, the steps of the Bachelor de Mirueña and of Gaspar de la Misericordia, who are coming with the confessor. I hide my papers under the bed and lie back down after tightening the cord of my gown, my hands pressed together, my body stiff, as if already lying in the royal scpulcher. I have reached the supreme hour of speaking. I will speak at length. I still have strength for that. I will tell all. I will tell it all, from beginning to end. All.

nd yet, placed in the inevitable position of having to speak, the moment of truth having arrived, I put on the mask of the one I wished to be but was not: the mask that will become my death mask—the last of the countless masks that I have worn through my existence with its uncertain beginning. Now that the mystery is upon me, I approach—after four journeys as an argonaut and one as a penitent—the terrible moment of delivery of arms, pomp, and rags. And they want me to talk. But now the words stick in my throat. To tell all, to relate everything, would be to weaken my position—"to give without return," as they say in the language of barter—among the men of faith, of shared belief, who have been magnanimous and consoling. And so it was that I took for my own—I who from ambition disregarded the laws of my people—those strictures dictated, on the eve of his death, to Moses, who like me was of uncertain birth, and, like me, was an announcer of Promised Lands: "You shall plant vineyards and dress them, but you shall neither drink of the wine nor gather the grapes; for the worm shall eat them. You shall have olive trees throughout all your territory, but you shall not anoint yourself with the oil; for your olives shall drop off." And Yahweh also said to that visionary of distant lands: "You shall see the land before you; but you shall not go there." . . . It is no longer a time to guard my words. Let my confession be reduced to what I want to reveal. Like Jason, who, in the tragedy of *Medea,* told what it suited him to tell in the language of a good dramatic poet, the language of passion and honor, full of cries for greater indulgence, and nothing more. Now I see myself extricated from the labyrinth in which I was lost. I wanted to gird the earth, but the earth was too large for me. It is for others to clear away the transcendental enigmas the earth still holds for us, starting from the port at one end of the coast of Cuba that I called the *Alpha-Omega* to signify that there, before me, one empire ended and another began; there an age ended, and another commenced.

. . . And now the confessor searches for my face in the recesses of the pillows soaked with the sweat of my fever, looking into my eyes. He raises the curtain on the final scene. The moment of truth, the final reckoning. But there will be no reckoning. I will say only *what could be inscribed in marble* about me. From my mouth comes the voice of *the other* who often has inhabited me. He will know what to say: "May the heavens have mercy on me, and weep upon the land."

III

THE SHADOW

Tu non dimandi

chè spiriti son queste chc

tu vedi?

Dante, The Inferno, IV

You do not ask

what spirits are these

you see before you?

nvisible — without weight, without dimension, casting no shadow, an errant transparency who had lost all sense of the vulgar notions of hot and cold, day and night, good and evil — he had spent several hours wandering within Bernini's quadruple colonnade, before the massive doors of Saint Peter's were opened. The man who had so often navigated without maps gave only a scornful glance at the many tourists who, every day, consult their guides and Baedekers before getting lost in the basilica, and then he headed directly toward the most famous marvels within that palace of marvels, which, for him, today, would be a palace of justice. Tried in absentia, a man on paper, his image evoked, his voice issuing from other mouths that will attack or defend him: now, almost four centuries after his death, they were examining every minor passage of his life, deciding whether he should be considered a supreme hero — as his panegyrists believed — or an ordinary human being, subject to all the weaknesses of his condition, which is how he was portrayed by certain rationalist historians, who were, perhaps, incapable of perceiving the *poetry of his actions* from behind their walls of papers, files, and chronicles. The moment of decision had arrived, when they would determine whether, in the future, he would merit statues with laudatory epigraphs or something more transcendent and universal than a bronze, stone, or marble image set in a public plaza. Not looking for a final judgment — that of the Sistine Chapel — which was not yet considering his case, he headed, with perfect aim, toward some rooms that were closed to the visiting public, in the Lipsonotec, whose curator, a learned Bollandist and, therefore, something of an osteologist, odontologist, and anat-

133

omist, was absorbed, as usual, in the examination, study, and classification of the innumerable bones, teeth, fingernails, hair, and other saintly relics that were stored in the drawers of desks and chests. Although the dead, in general, are not interested in the fate of their own bones, the Invisible Presence wanted to know if they had reserved some space in this place for the few bones that were left, just in case . . . "It seems we are going to have a rather splendid hearing," the curator said to a young seminarian, his disciple, who was being trained in the classification methods of the Lipsonotec. "That's because today's case is not a current one," the seminarian answered. "No decision on beatification is ever a current case," observed the curator, in the irritable tone that he always used, although it didn't seem to affect the other man. "True. But in the case being considered, the person is world famous. And the petition was introduced by two popes: first, Pius IX; now His Holiness Leo XIII." "Pius IX died before the ten years had passed that are required for the Holy Congregation of Rites to begin the examination of the documents and justifying arguments." "Even though the case of Christopher Columbus was introduced at the same time, Count Roselly de Lorgues applied for two other halos: one for Joan of Arc; the other, for Louis XVI." "Look: the beatification of Joan of Arc seems quite likely, but that of Louis XVI is about as likely as your whore of an aunt's." "Thank you." "Not only that, we have to put a lid on these petitions. We are more than just a factory churning out holy pictures." There was a silence during which some flies entered, on an exploratory flight, as if looking for something they never found. "What do you think of Columbus's chances?" the seminarian asked. "Poor. In the pool the Swiss halberdiers have in their guardroom, the odds against Columbus this morning were five to one." "I think they're going to go down," said the younger man. "Why, did you bet on him?" "No. Because we don't have a single mariner saint. I've looked in *The Golden Legend,* the *Acta Sanctorum* by John Bolland, and even in *The Crowns of Martyrdom* by Prudentius, and I haven't found a single one. Seafarers don't have a patron saint who was one of them. Plenty of fishermen — starting with the ones on the Sea of Galilee. But a real saltwater sailor, not a single one." "True," said the curator, going over the lists in his head, the calendars, catalogs, and registers — "true, because Saint Christopher never had anything to do with sails. Boatman on a river, that's what Christo-phoros was, as we know, and because he carried on his shoulders, from one shore to the other, One who did not fear drowning in the turbulent waters, a date palm grew and flourished at the spot where Christopher planted his staff in solid ground." "Patron saint of all travelers, whether they travel by boat, burro, balloon, or railroad train . . ." They both started to thumb through cards and papers. And the Invisible Presence, looking over their shoulders, saw names and more names — some of which were completely unknown to him — of saints invoked by seafarers in time of storms, wrecks, and ill winds: Saint Vincent, deacon and martyr, because his body was once seen miraculously floating on a violent ocean, even though it was weighed down by an enormous stone ("But it wasn't his job," observed the seminarian); Saints Cosmas and Damian, Moorish saints — "our fatherland is Arabia," they said — because the proconsul of Lycia threw them in the ocean, tied together; Saint Clement, also thrown into the sea, whose body was found on an island near Chersonese, with an anchor attached to it ("They weren't sailors either," protested the youth); Saint Castreuse, for having defied a typhoon aboard a rolling ship ("He was on board in spite of himself"); Saint Leo, for his torment at the hands of some pirates ("That doesn't make him a sailor"); Saint Peter Gonzalez, better known as Saint Elmo ("He converted many sailors and lit Saint Elmo's Fire, which often dances so prettily at night on the tops of the masts. But he was a man from the interior of his country, he came from Astorga, whose delicious sugar-bread is famous all over Spain, because . . ."

"Let's not get off the subject," said the curator, "let's not get off the subject"). And he went on with the list: Saint Cuthbert, patron of Saxon mariners ("This smells to me like a Nordic saga . . . A sailor from Cadíz or Marseilles isn't going to pray to a Viking"); the Archangel Raphael ("How could an archangel wear a sailor cap, tell me that!"); Nicholas, bishop of Mira, who, invisible, repaired the mast on a pilgrim ship and steered it to safe port ("But he's better known today for steering a sleigh and delivering toys, than for traveling on water"). "Well, then, we're screwed," said the Curator of the Vatican Lipsonotec. "Because of Saint Dominic of Lores, and Saint Valerius, and Saint Anthony of Padua, and Saint Restitutus, and Saint Raymond, and Saint Budoc (I've never even heard of him!), all of them invoked by sailors, though none of them was ever a sailor." "Conclusion: Pius IX was right. We need a Saint Christopher Columbus." "I would have to prepare a box to store his relics." "The bad thing is that these roving men don't leave many relics." "So there isn't as much as a femur, a metacarpal, a kneecap, or a finger or toe of his left?" "That's another feud. And one that will never be settled, since those bones have been disturbed, disarranged, disjointed, discussed, dislocated, and disputed, like no other bones." And summarizing the results of recent research, motivated by today's petition, the learned Bollandist explained to his disciple that Columbus, having died in Valladolid, had been buried in the Franciscan convent in that city. But in 1513, his remains were moved to the monastery of Las Cuevas in Seville, only to be disinterred thirty-three years later and transported to Santo Domingo, where they remained until 1795. But wouldn't you know, the blacks of the French group on the island suddenly had a change of heart and started huge fires, burning the haciendas and slitting the throats of their masters. The Spanish authorities, fearful that the flames of rebellion might spread, dispatched the mortal remains of the Grand Admiral to Havana, in whose cathedral they stayed until

they could be returned to Santo Domingo, where there were
plans to erect a splendid mausoleum, with sculptures, allegories,
and everything: something fit for the renowned remains . . .
But, in the meantime, he said, the plot took a twist that was
almost Rochambeaulian, if I can mention Rochambeau in the
halls of the Vatican. "You forget, sir, that here everyone, from
the high to the low, has read the adventures of Rochambeau."
"Christopher Columbus was not alone in the cathedral on
Santo Domingo: his funeral urn was near the urns of his
firstborn son, Diego; Diego's son, Don Louis Columbus, the
first Duke of Veragua; and Diego's brother, Don Christopher
Columbus II. And they say what happened was that on the tenth
of September in 1877, an architect who was making some repairs
on the cathedral discovered a metal box on which there was an
abbreviated inscription: *D of A. Fst. Ad. C.C.A.* –which he
interpreted as: *Discoverer of America. First Admiral. Christopher
Columbus Admiral.* Then the remains moved to Havana *are not*
those of the man we are going to beatify . . ." "If that happens,"
murmured the seminarian. "But–and here is the tragedy–
inside the metal box is written, in German gothic characters:
The Illustrious and Esteemed Gentleman Don Christopher Columbus,
with nothing about 'Admiral.' And the fuckers started to say that
those weren't the remains of Columbus I, but of Columbus II,
and that those of Columbus I were in Cuba, and then a Venezuelan published a notorious pamphlet that stirred up the dispute,
and that set the stage for a worse battle than the one over the
Filioque . . . The result: no one knows whether these are the
bones of Columbus I and not of Columbus II, or if they're those
of Columbus II and not of Columbus I, and no one is asking me,
it will be resolved in the Holy Congregation of Rites, which was
established for that, because not so much as a single clavicle, a
radiale, an ulna that has not been duly authenticated as from
Columbus will enter here. This is a serious Lipsonotec, and it
can't accept vertebrae, parietals, occipitals, or metatarsals from

just anyone, because there are categories for everything. And as for me, I'm not going to play the game of eeeny-meeny-miny-mo." "Here, you can't buy your way in with gold after you're dead," agreed the seminarian. "Even though, according to Marx, Columbus said that *gold is a marvelous thing. He who has gold can have anything he desires. Using gold, souls can even open the gates of paradise.*" "Columbus certainly said that; but don't quote Columbus by way of Marx. You shouldn't even say that name where walls have ears. You know that since the publication of the *Syllabus* certain books are frowned upon here." "But still it seems that you know Marx just as well as you know Rochambeau." "Son, I have to: I'm on the *Index* Commission." "I see that you don't get terribly bored concocting the *Index,*" said the seminarian, with a sly smile. "That explains why *Mademoiselle Maupin* and *Nana* are on the *Index.*" "Instead of all this bullshitting, let's go see how the beatification of the Grand Admiral is going," said the furious Bollandist, just missing the seminarian with a kick of his buckled shoe. "That's right!" thought the Invisible One, "Right!" And, suddenly anxious, he hurried off, down corridors and up stairways, to the room where, at a call from the ushers, a solemn Morality Play would be presented, with him as its absent/present protagonist.

The majestic actors in the Morality Play entered from stage left and stage right and seated themselves, in an order that observed hierarchy, rank, and function, around an enormous table covered with a crimson silk cloth, each of the actors assuming the medieval aspect of a member of the Holy Office by gestures and attitudes remembered from very old ceremonies. In the center were seated the president and the two judges who made up the collegial tribunal; at one end of the table, the promoter of the faith, critic of the canonization, the Devil's Advocate, and at the other end of the table, the Postulator of canonization — in this case, not Roselly de Lorgues, who had died a few years before, but the erudite Genoan merchant José Baldi, expert on precious stones, well-respected and esteemed within the Vatican for his many acts of charity. The chief civil clerk of the Congregation of Rites, with his assistant, sat in between. Folios and sheaves of papers made their appearance from within satchels and brief-cases, and after a prayer imploring the Holy Spirit to inspire them to make fair decisions and appropriate sentences, the judicial process began. . . The Invisible One felt his invisible ears prick up and hold still, like those of a wolf who senses danger, alert to all that would be said in this tribunal, which had been reconvened after such a long adjournment to consider the question of the beatification that, over the course of time, had accumulated more than the favor of the six hundred-odd bishops who had signed the first petition, so that now eight hundred sixty had put their signatures at the bottom of the third petition—which would most likely be the final one. The president asked the Postulator to swear an oath to abstain from fraud at all times, to adhere to the truths he honestly believed in his soul and conscience in creating his arguments in defense of the cause. Speaking deliberately, drawing a breath between each of his phrases, separating his adjectives, carefully putting the cap-stone to each paragraph he constructed, José Baldi made an impressive summary of the case Count Roselly de Lorgues had expounded, with profuse appendices and preliminary docu-ments, in the book commissioned by Pope Pius IX. As this discourse piled on the dithyrambs and vocatives, the Invisible One felt a sweet pleasure. In the face of this portrait of excellent qualities, of virtues, of masculine piety, of generosity, of disin-terestedness and interior greatness; this portrait of miracles he had performed, although with the modesty and humility of a mendicant friar; in the face of proof that he had possessed supernatural powers that he had never even guessed he had, how could his judges hesitate? When, like Saint Clement who quieted tempests, like Saint Luis Beltran, an American who

made apostolic visits to Colombia, Panama, and the Antilles—
his Antilles—he had wrested thousands upon thousands of
Indians from the utter darkness of their idolatries, and when,
just like Saint Patrick—Baldi said—*"apostle to verdant Ireland, who
heard the unborn in their mothers' womb calling him to Ireland, so he,
Christopher Columbus, during the eighteen terrible years he wasted in
useless efforts, had borne in his soul the incredible clamor of half the
world's population . . ."* He was laying a magnificent ground-
work. And so great was the Postulator's enthusiasm that the
Invisible One began to be impressed with himself: he discovered that what he had attributed to the powerful effect of
another's faith was actually his own work, the action of his own
hands, of his privileged will, of his power *to ask* and *to receive;* and
the most extraordinary thing was that, according to a certain
Leon Bloy, who was frequently quoted by José Baldi in his
panegyric, Columbus's miracles surpassed those—simpler and
more limited, if you looked at them properly—of healing the
sick, making the lame walk, the dumb speak, and reviving a few
dead. No. *I think of Moses,* said Leon Bloy, *I think of Moses, because
Columbus reveals all Creation, divides the world among the kings of the
earth, talks to God in the Tempest, and the result of his plea is the
patrimony of all mankind.* "Olé!" exclaims the Devil's Advocate,
drumming his hands on the table as if he were accompanying a
flamenco dancer, "olé and olé!" But his voice is drowned out by
the Postulator: *Count Roselly de Lorgues didn't hesitate to put the
Grand Admiral in the line that ran from Noah to Abraham, Moses,
John the Baptist, and Saint Peter, granting him the supreme title of
Ambassador of God.* (Oh, wonderful, wonderful, wonderful
Christophoros, you've won the game, your halo is waiting in the
wings, you will have a consistory, you will have altars everywhere, you will be like the giant Atlas whose powerful shoulders support the world that became round forever, thanks to
you; you made it round where it had been flat, limited, circum-
scribed, and you surrounded it with the bottomless abyss of a

firmament that was *also underneath it,* an identical and parallel firmament, so that no one can know for sure whether up is down or down is up! . . .) And when José Baldi ended his speech, the enthusiasm of the Invisible One reached its peak, and, like an ocean mist, invisible tears of gratitude began to form in his invisible eyes, at the shadows of the witnesses the Postulator had invited to make their statements, before the skeptical smile—why was he so skeptical?—of the Devil's Advocate, whose job was to wear such disturbing smiles on his diabolical face. "And is there no ordinary judge here, or, lacking that, an ecclesiastical delegate?" the Devil's Advocate inquired. The president answered him drily: "Idle question. It's true that whenever a *normal beatification proceeding* is being held, only an ordinary judge is allowed to officiate, or else a dignitary who enjoys episcopal jurisdiction over the place where the person whose life is being examined died, or where he worked miracles . . ." "Who is called the *Local Bishop,*" noted the Devil's Advocate. "Don't lecture us about something we already know perfectly well," said the president severely. "But on this point, I believe we should again refer to Count Roselly de Lorgues: *Neither the local bishop of the place he was born*—he tells us—*nor the local bishop of the place he died can appear in court in this case . . .*" "I believe it would be a little difficult . . ." "*The remarkable navigator moved to Genoa at the age of fourteen,*" continued the president. "*He died in Valladolid, while visiting there, and his remains were moved elsewhere. His legal residence was in Córdoba, but he never went there. He had an official residence on Santo Domingo, but he was continually absent from it. Thus no bishop is in a position to supply us with any information.*" "Fine, we already knew that nobody lives four hundred years . . ." "It seems to me that with that statement you impugn the reliability of the scriptures," said the chief clerk quickly, seeming to come awake at this point, "because, in fact . . . In the fifth chapter of Genesis we are told that Seth lived 912 years, that Enoch lived 815, that Quenan reached 910

and then died." "Phew! About time, too!" exclaimed the Devil's
Advocate, provoking a few barely suppressed laughs from the
acolyte and the two adjunct judges. "Order. Order," said the
president. "All I ask is that to save time we skip to the Deluge,"
said Beelzebub's lawyer. "Someone made that joke before you
did, the French poet Racine." "In the comedy *Les Plaideurs,"* the
chief clerk pointed out. "I see you know your classics," said the
always cunning minister of Belial. "But, to return to Columbus:
if he died in Valladolid, why didn't the bishop from there leave
some written testimony we could rely on?" "The Bishop of
Vallalodid would scarcely be informed of the death of a poor
stranger, tired and sick, who happened to get stuck in his city,"
said Baldi. "And is there no written testimony from a local
bishop somewhere he worked miracles?" "I'm tired of repeating," said the Postulator, "that the miracles Columbus performed were of a *unique type, unlike most miracles. We could say that
they are not located in any particular place; they are universal."* "I can
see that the pontifical decree got here by an *unusual route,"* said
the Devil's Advocate in a sharp voice. "Caiaphas!" cried a voice
behind the Invisible One. He turned to see a hairy man, his face
almost hidden by a dense hedge of a beard, smelling rather foul,
who had rolled his eyes, which were inflamed with anger, under
bushy eyebrows, crying: "Caiaphas! Caiaphas!" The Devil's
Advocate now took aim at José Baldi: "The Postulator's panegyric rests entirely on the book by Roselly de Lorgues, which,
as I understand it, is a work of honest intentions, but which is
terribly biased and lacks historical rigor. And the best proof is
that a prize of thirty thousand pesetas has just been created to be
awarded to the best biography — solidly documented, credible,
modern — in an open contest intended as a general commem-
oration of the quadricentennial of the Discovery of America,
which will take place shortly. And do you know who has created
this prize, out of dissatisfaction with the book by Roselly de
Lorgues? None other than the very illustrious Duke of Veragua,

Marquis of Jamaica, Governor of the Indies, Senator of the Kingdom, and three times Grandee of Spain, the only direct descendant of Christopher Columbus." "The miserable wretch!" howled the hairy little man, who, fired by his indignation, had leaped over two rows of chairs, falling at the side of the Invisible One. "The ingrate! A trainer of bulls for the ring, who sells them to add some excitement to circus games, while he doesn't have the balls to be a torero, to confront his own herd. He prefers to peek out at his bulls from the hallway the bull-fighters use to escape from the plaza, because he breeds vicious bulls so that they will kill the most fighters." "The prize of thirty thousand pesetas. . ." continued the advocate. "Are the thirty denarii of Judas!" screamed Leon Bloy, the eternal terror, whom the Invisible One had now identified. "Silence!" shouted the president, "or I will call the Swiss Guard." "Whatever new history will be written," the Postulator went on, "it will in no way diminish the greatness, the obvious sanctity, of this amazing cosmographer, of whom Schiller said: *Proceed without fear, Christopher. If what you are looking for has not yet been created, God will make it appear in the world, from nothing, to justify your audacity.*" "He wasn't such a great cosmographer," said the Devil's Advocate, "or not according to Victor Hugo." And at this point it seemed to the Invisible One that Victor Hugo leaned on the bar and said: *If Christopher Columbus had been a good cosmographer, he never would have discovered the New World.* (But I had the nose of a sailor, which is worth any and all cosmographies, murmured the Invisible One.) "And to bring in Victor Hugo, who never sailed any farther than the Isle of Guernsey, to tell us about seafaring!" roared Leon Bloy through the thicket of his beard. And now—a theatrical coup!—Jules Verne entered the bar, looking like Robur the Conqueror, and with all his aplomb. "This is the last straw!" someone exclaimed, protesting forcibly. "A charlatan! Why not call Phileas Fogg and the sons of Captain Grant, too?" "It's enough that you've called the father of the sons of Captain

Grant," said Jules Verne with dignity. And he continued: *The truth is that a group of facts, systems, and doctrines was being developed during Columbus's era. It was time for a single intelligence to come and propound and assimilate them. All these disparate ideas came together in the mind of a single man who possessed, in the highest degree, the genius of perseverance and of audacity.* "What about Providence?" asked Leon Bloy. "Where does this wretch leave Divine Providence?" But the novelist didn't seem to hear him: *Columbus had been on an Island* . . . and possibly on Greenland.* (An Island, yes; but I was never in Greenland, muttered the Invisible One.) *During the entire voyage, the Admiral was careful to hide from his companions the true distance they had traveled each day.* "If he imagined it did any good . . ." mumbled Bloy. *Until the cry of "Land" was sounded! But the true glory of Columbus was not that he reached land, but that he set sail.* "Imbecile! Captain Nemo!" yelled Bloy. But now Verne's speech became as dry and precise as that of a mathematics professor: *Through this voyage, the Old World assumed responsibility for the moral and political education of the New World. But how could it rise to this task, burdened with so many narrow-minded ideas, semibarbaric impulses, odious religious doctrines? . . . Columbus immediately began to take Indians captive, with the intention of selling them in Spain.* "I call to the attention of the tribunal the fact that Columbus *instituted* slavery in the New World," the Devil's Advocate cried triumphantly. (The Invisible One felt his invisible body turn cold, as cold as the icy advocate's in any season.) *He swore that the Indians were cannibals. But the navigator did not encounter cannibals in Baracoa or anywhere else.* "That's what we wanted to get to," the agent of Beelzebub said, bad-temperedly. "And I ask permission of the tribunal to introduce Father Bartolomé de las Casas to testify to that charge." ("I'm screwed," moaned the Invisible One, "now I'm really

---

*Columbus's visit to Iceland is "possible though uncertain," according to Menéndez Pidal.

screwed.") And he was already coming in, the bald, ascetic Jacobin, his forehead wrinkled in a frown so he looked just like one of Zurbarán's monks, appraising the tribunal with a look both gloomy and hard. "Atrabilious megalomaniac! Trickster!" shrieked Leon Bloy, his fury at its peak. And immediately a chorus of reproaches sprang up from some others who came tumbling into the room. "Hypochondriac! Opportunist! Falsifier! Calumniator! Big bag of bile! Serpent in sandals! . . ." "*You will be giving your testimony in vain!*" blared one, in a voice like a bugle in a ballroom. "Absalom! Ugolino! Judas Iscariot! Scum of the earth!" shouted the rest of them. "Who are these agitators?" asked the president. "They are Objectors to the Black Legend of the Spanish conquest," explained the chief clerk. "There are a lot of them these days . . ." "Silence! Or I will have to throw out the troublemakers," said the president. Then, seeing that order had been restored: "What proof do we have that the Indians were cannibals? I accept what Father Bartolomé claimed: *To start, I will say that the Indians belong to a superior race, as far as beauty, intelligence, and creativity . . . They fulfill Aristotle's six essential conditions to form a perfect republic, which is sufficient unto itself.* ("Now he's going to tell us that they built the Parthenon and gave us Roman Law!" Leon Bloy exclaimed.) "But did they or didn't they eat human flesh?" asked the president. *Not everywhere, although it is true that one will find instances in Mexico, but more for religious reasons than for other causes. But Herodotus, Pomponius Mela, and even Saint Jerome tell us that there were anthropophagi among the Scythians, Masagetas, and Scots.* "Long live the cannibals! Long live the cannibals!" the shout went up, with Leon Bloy and the Objectors to the Black Legend crying in unison. "If there were cannibals among the Indians in America," said the Devil's Advocate imperturbably, "that's twice the reason Columbus had for not bringing the Indians to Spain, because the cannibals would present a constant danger to the children playing in the public gardens. And it could have meant that some Indian would get a craving for the loins of a pretty little girl." "I call the attention of the tribunal to the absurd allegations of the Devil's Advocate," said the Postulator. "Prosecutor, withdraw these 'loins of a pretty little girl,'" said the president, furrowing his brow. "I withdraw the loins and the pretty little girl is left with a bone," said the Devil's Advocate. "Now let's see if the prosecution witness can provide us with proof that the postulant deliberately instituted slavery among the American Indians," said the president. *Suffice it to say that when Queen Isabella, who is glorious in our memory, learned that Columbus's men were selling American slaves in the market in Seville, she flew into a rage and asked: "WHAT POWER HAS MY ADMIRAL TO GIVE AWAY MY VASSALS?" And she ordered that a public announcement be made in Granada and Seville that all those in Castile who were given Indians by the Admiral must return them to their place of origin in the first ships departing, or face a penalty of death.* Now José Baldi asked to have a word and began to speak in dulcet tones, in a conciliatory manner: "The eminent French philosopher Saint-Bonnet . . ." "He was my teacher," murmured Leon Bloy. ". . . in his treatise *Misery*, wrote, at the end of Chapter XXIX, these words that I submit for your consideration: *Slavery was a school of patience, meekness, abnegation. Only Pride prevents Grace from entering the soul, and it is Humility that removes this obstacle and opens its path. Therefore, in his wisdom, ancient man considered slavery something like a necessary school of patience and resignation, which brought the slave closer to Renouncing Satan, to the soul's virtue, and to the moral goal of Christianity."* "Long live *chains!*" shouted the Devil's Advocate. "I ask leave of the president of this tribunal to remind everyone that while we don't live in the days of Ferdinand VII of Spain, this lawsuit takes us back to the days of the Catholic kings," said the chief clerk, waking up, and then, as soon as he had spoken, falling back into a sound sleep. "Since we are in the days of the Catholic kings, all the more reason to point out that Queen Isabella, in her famous codicil of 1504, *asked and then ordered her husband and his children not to consent to the molestation of the Indian inhabitants and dwellers of the Indies, in either their goods or their persons, that they be well and justly treated."* José Baldi addressed the tribunal urgently: "Just a minute . . . Just a minute . . . It's interesting to call attention to the fact that the Catholic queen *ordered her husband and his children,* not the Admiral to whom she gave no instructions in this regard . . ." "Ingenious!" exclaimed the Devil's Advocate. "Very ingenious! Almost as ingenious as Christopher Columbus's Egg!" ("He has pulled that one out already," muttered the Invisible One.) José Baldi threw up his arms with feigned disgust. "That childish story! That nonsense! Columbus with his superhuman dignity would never have stooped to that kind of foolishness! Voltaire himself . . ." ("Oh oh, if he brings Voltaire into this, I'm burned!" moaned the Invisible One.) ". . . Voltaire himself, before Washington Irving, explained that the famous Egg of Columbus was really the Egg of Brunelleschi . . ." ("So now we've got two of them! . . .") "The genial architect used this sally, which was good for livening up dessert, to explain how he had conceived the design of the cupola of Santa Maria del Fiore." ("This is getting better! . . .") "I would have to see if . . ." "Let's not fight over one egg, more or less," said the president, "and let's return, please, to the question of slavery." Father Bartolomé stood up in front of the tribunal again: *I am quite certain that if he had not been prevented by the great adversities that befell him, he would very quickly have removed all the people from all the islands, because he was so determined to load them in the ships he had brought from Castile and from the Azores, so he could sell them as slaves wherever he could find acceptance.* This time Leon Bloy faced the president: "You are prosecuting his intentions . . . *I am quite certain . . . I am quite certain . . .* How much credence can we give to the suppositions of this humbug?" "Columbus has been thrown to the beasts!" clamored the Objectors. "Savage! Barbarian!" spat out the Devil's Advocate, laughing, and he made a fist with the thumb pointing downward. "Is there any proof that Columbus established slavery deliberately?" asked the president. "Because there is some evidence that it was his brother who was guilty of sending the Indians to Spain. Was the Grand Admiral informed of this fact?" "I should say so! Informed enough to write a letter to this fine brother of his, recommending that he *overload his ships with slaves* and take *a fair share* off the profits made by their sale." "Who saw this letter?" asked Baldi. And the Bishop of Chiapas answered in a firm voice: *I saw it, and it was his hand and his signature.* "Worm! Perjurer! Imposter! Pharisee!" shouted Leon Bloy with such force that he almost split his throat and ended up out of breath. *Whoever steals the fruit of another's sweat is like a man who kills his neighbor,* shouted Father Bartolomé de las Casas in a terrible voice. "Who's quoting Marx?" asked the chief clerk, shaken out of his sound sleep. "Chapter 34 of Ecclesiastes," declared the Bishop of Chiapas . . . "Let's drop this, and move on to the question of the morality of the postulant," said the president. "I ask the court's permission to introduce the poet Alphonse Lamartine, as witness for the prosecution," said the Devil's Advocate. ("What kind of crap will the man who wrote *Le Lac* tell us about maritime matters?" grunted Leon Bloy under his breath.) Self-important in his tribunal frock coat, a lock of hair draped across his forehead, Lamartine quickly became embroiled in a long explanation, the only part of which the pained Invisible One could understand was the reference to *his wicked habits and his bastard son.* "That's enough," said the Devil's Advocate. "Because it brings us to one of the most serious issues that we have to consider here: the Admiral's illegitimate relations with a certain Beatriz who was—and this is public knowledge—his, I won't say mistress or concubine or lover, so as not to insult the memory of that woman, rather, I'll use the delicate term favored in the Spanish classics, and call her *his beloved.*" (At the sound of the name Beatriz, the Invisible One was visibly moved, and he made his own the strophe Dante used to express his emotion when he saw Beatrice appear on the banks of Lethe: *the ice that had hardened in my heart turned into sighs and tears, flowing from my heart, forced through my eyes and mouth . . .*) The Postulator, Baldi, got to his feet, asking, with an exasperated gesture, to be recognized: "What we're dealing with here is no more than slinging mud at a perfectly human, but pure love . . . Yes, esteemed solicitor for the devil, stop making that sign that is only fit for a muleteer with your irreverent hand, so you can listen better to what Count Roselly de Lorgues tells us about the autumnal idyll of this great man: *In spite of the fact that he was forty-some years old, a widower, poor, with a foreign accent, and gray hair, a young woman of great nobility and rare beauty chose to be his companion. Her name was Beatriz and in her were united all the virtue and refinement of a Cordoban woman. But this ray of light who came to bring a little joy to his troubled heart did not deter him for an instant from the mission he was destined to perform . . ."* "Shouldn't some violins accompany this pathetic romance?" asked the Devil's Advocate insolently. "Settle down!" cried the president. "This young woman, a model of virtue, whom the great man loved and respected . . ." "He respected her so much he gave her a son," Lucifer's lawyer let loose, rather crudely. "And Columbus felt so responsible for this little pecadillo that he sought to offer some consolation for the sadness and loneliness of the widow saddled with a little Cordoban son, and that is why when Rodrigo de Triana gave the famous cry, 'Land! Land!' he might just as well have shouted: 'What a romantic tangle!'. . ." "Let's not talk about Rodrigo de Triana and the question of the ten thousand maravedis, which were better off in the hands of a young mother, than in those of any sailor, who would have gambled them away in the first tavern . . ." ("Yes, yes, yes . . . Let Rodrigo de Triana rest in peace, because after they finished with him they'd drag in Pinzon and my servants, Salcedo and Arroyal, who, in my absence, told the cursed Biscayan Juan de la Cosa about my secret maps, and then I'll really be beaten.") And now the Devil's Advocate, with a diabolical smile, brought the debate to a diabolical close with this poisonous remark: "Apparently the sons of love—by which I mean love made flesh in a bridal bed that has not been sanctified—are the object of a very special affection on the part of the parents. So that Christopher Columbus always showed a marked predilection for his illegitimate son, Don Fernando . . . But the fact that this father felt a particular love for a son conceived out of wedlock hardly makes him a fit person to assume the aureole of sainthood . . . Because if it did, there would be so many haloes lighting up the world that every night would be as bright as day." "That would be a magnificent system of public illumination," stated the chief clerk, who had given more than one sign of mental weakness during the trial. "It would be much better than the one invented by that Yankee Edison, who, as a matter of fact, made the first electric light the same year that His Holiness Pope Pius IX died, after he introduced the first petition to canonize the Grand Admiral." *"Fiat lux!"* the president said conclusively. And the images began to fade away: Bartolomé de las Casas, Victor Hugo, Lamartine, Jules Verne. And the Objectors to the Black Legend of the Spanish conquest disappeared—this time without an untimely outburst. The tenuous mists, made up of phantasmagorical shapes, which obscured the Invisible One's vision of the room, began to dissipate. And the figures of the tribunal came into focus, with the clarity of a drawing, in front of a large oil painting showing the martyrdom of Saint Sebastian, pierced by arrows. The president rose: "Has the chief clerk made a record of all we have seen and heard?" (The chief clerk answered in the affirmative, regarding the scraps of paper he had arranged, smallest to largest, on the green blotter at his place—a tiny green meadow on the red silk of the table. The acolyte made a discreet gesture, and everyone understood that he was the one who had taken it all down . . .) "After everything is said and done," continued the president, "two major charges still stand against the postulant Columbus: the first, extremely serious, of having a mistress — all the more inexcusable when we consider that the navigator was a widower when he met the woman who gave him a child — and the second, no less serious, of having instituted and promoted an inexcusable slave trade, selling, in public markets, several hundred Indians captured in the New World . . . In view of these transgressions, this tribunal will have to make a final decision regarding whether the said Columbus, postulated for beatification, merits the great opportunity such beatification opens for him, access to canonization, which proceeds without debate." The chief clerk's acolyte circulated a small black urn in which each member of the tribunal placed a folded paper. The president then uncovered the urn and proceeded to the tally. "Only one vote in favor," he said. "Therefore, the motion is denied." Still José Baldi protested, futilely citing Roselly de Lorgues: *Columbus was a saint; a saint offered by the will of the Lord where Satan was king.* "Shouting will accomplish nothing," the promoter of the faith said with irony: "It is over." They packed up their notebooks, folios, and bundles of paper, the president adjusted his skullcap as a breeze suddenly filtered through the room, and the Devil's Advocate disappeared like Mephistopheles through a trap door in an opera by Gounod. His beard shaking from rage, Leon Bloy rushed to the exit, snorting: *The Holy Congregation of Rites never had an inkling of the grandeur of this project. Little it cared for a providential mission! From the moment that the Cause deviated from the ordinary, instead of established fact, weighed, signed, certified, and sealed with episcopal wax, everyone became uneasy and worked to prevent that cause from progressing. And, moreover, for them . . . what kind of genius was this Christopher Columbus? Nothing but a sailor. And what has the Holy Congregation of Rites ever cared for maritime matters?** "I'm screwed," the Invisible One murmured, leaving his seat to make for the main door, on a path that would take him, after a long passage

*Leon Bloy, *The Revealer of the Globe,* chapter 10.

through corridors and galleries, outside the immense edifice-
city. Before leaving the building, he cast a last look at the picture
that showed the martyrdom of Saint Sebastian: "Like you, I
have been pierced . . . But the arrows that have entered me
were propelled, after all, from the bows of the Indians of the
New World whom I tried to chain and sell."

As if fascinated by a sudden coincidence of images, he stopped
and paused to consider that painting depicting the torment of a
saint killed by arrows, which made him think of still other
arrows — cruel and delicious arrows — that, since mythological
times, have fatefully wounded their targets, causing the ineffable
agony of lovers whirled in the "hellish storm" that eternally
moves Paolo and Francesca, yesterday, today, and tomorrow.
(When I committed the sin of concubinage by not marrying my
Beatriz, whom I so loved, leaving my seed in her fertile field, I
did not foresee those ferocious observers of the canon gathering
to condemn me, those icy clerics elected to the Vatican through
sinecure and indifference, opposing me as if they were sitting at
the right hand of God to judge men, for having, like the magnificent cavaliers of knight errancy [and what was I, if not a knight
errant of the sea?], taking as my woman one whom I never
betrayed in spirit while living united in the flesh with the one
who would perpetuate my line. And as I listened, from the
heights of a court decked out for legal trickery, I listened to those
ordained personages, grim and contentious, discuss *my case,* I
heard more than once that the heart has its reasons — who said
that? — that the mind knows not. And I suddenly thought of the
prostrate and sorrowful figure of the Page of Sigüenza, who also
had a mistress, the guide and beacon of his destiny, like the noble
Lady Madrigal of the High Towers . . . Taking to his heart —
like Amadis with the peerless Oriana — the one he had seen for
the first time in the Moclín camp, after the taking of Illora, he
loved her with the same devotion in which he had until then
held his sweetheart from Sigüenza. And, with her image in

mind, moved by the same pledge that motivated his Mistress in her glorious zeal of reconquest, perhaps to increase in fame and bravery in her eyes, he launched a headlong attack, and fell in the crusade against the Moors and was cast in a marble statue, wrapped in his military cape, his flowing hair in an Italian style—the cross of Santiago red on his chest like an eternal sprout from his bloody heart.* How I envied the page, more a warrior than I, although he was depicted on the lid of his tomb reading a book—a book that might have been by Seneca the Elder, while I, seeking the clear prophesies within his *Medea,* translated prophetic verses of the other Seneca! . . . You and I— and why deny that I was once jealous of you?—loved the same woman, although you never knew, as I did [Or perhaps? . . . who can be sure? How can one penetrate such a shrouded mystery?] the unequaled pleasure of holding a queen in your arms. Madrigal of the High Towers was our incomparable Oriana, although *those who judge me,* dusty magistrates, full of canonical self-righteousness, could not understand the constancy of a pledge held in secret, because it was necessary that no one know about it, that both of us keep quiet about what perhaps led you to sacrifice yourself in a meritorious display of honor, while I, following the sentiment that after a certain time was always the compass and guide of my actions, did not reject Beatriz, my Beatriz whom I loved just the same. There are rules of gentlemanly fidelity that these mediocre shysters who now find me guilty of concubinage, fornication, and who knows what else will never understand . . . If I had not been devoted to the ideal that I pursued, I would have lain with Indians—many of whom were quite desirable in their Edenic nakedness—as did so many, so many, of those who accompanied me in my discoveries . . . But that, that they can never accuse me of, however much they rummage through old papers, examine archives, or lend their ears to the slanders of Martín Pinzón, Juan de la Cosa, Rodrigo

---

*"The most beautiful statue in the world," said Ortega y Gasset.

de Triana, and other filthy scoundrels intent on staining my memory . . . In my life there came one surpassing moment when, setting my sights high, very high, I abandoned the lust of my body and ennobled my mind with a complete communion of spirit and flesh, and a new light illuminated the darkness of wayward actions and thoughts . . .)

nd the invisible one, stricken with anguish, found himself once again in the piazza of Saint Peter's . . . (By his side, sullen and hurried, passed the seminarian of the Lipsonotec, mumbling: "Never a day of rest here. No sooner am I finished with Columbus than they think of beatifying Joan of Arc, whose bones are also lost, since her ashes were scattered by the winds of Rouen . . . And I'll have to convince the chief clerk of that, since he thinks Joan of Arc was strangled in the Tower of London . . . What a job, my God! . . .") Soon another Invisible One joined the first — visible to him — his chest bare, carrying the trident of Poseidon, as he appeared to posterity in the famous portrait by Bronzino. Thus the Grand Admiral of Isabella and Ferdinand met, for the first time, his countryman and his near contemporary — give or take a few years — Andrea Doria, the Grand Admiral of Venice and Genoa. Both admirals, both Genoans, they began to converse amiably in their peculiar dialect. "I got bored in my sepulcher in the Church of San Mateo, so I came to take the air in this plaza," Andrea said. "Along the way I picked up a wad of tobacco. Care for a chew? No? That's funny, considering that you're more or less responsible for so many people snorting snuff, smoking pipes, and firing up Havanas in this country. Without you, we never would have known about tobacco." "Amerigo Vespucci would have acquainted people with it anyway," said Christopher, bitterly. "How did you get here from Genoa?" "By train. The Ventimiglia express." "And they let you get on the car like that — like that, practically naked, like Neptune in a mythological allegory?" "Don't forget that you and I dwell in the realm of the Invisibles. We're the Transparent Ones.

There are many like us, who, because of their fame, because people keep talking about them, cannot disappear into their transparency, removed from this screwed-up world where they put up statues of us, where new historians knock themselves out trying to bring to light the worst secrets of our private lives." "You're telling me!" "Sure. Lots of people don't know that we often travel by train or ship, with the Greek Aspasia, the knight Roland, Fra Angelico, or the Marquis of Santillana." "All those who have died become invisible." "But if they are cited and talked about for what they did and what they were, the Invisible Ones 'are made man,' as they say, and they begin to talk with those who call their names. Of course, there are, as always, different levels according to different degrees of demand. There are the *Class A* Invisibles, like Charlemagne or Philip II; *Class B*, like the Princess of Eboli or the knight Bayard; and there are the occasionals, much less solicited, like that unfortunate Visigoth king, Favila, mentioned in the *Chronicle* of Alfonso III, of whom all that is known is that he ruled for two years and died when he was eaten by a bear, or, speaking of your world, that Bartolomé Cornejo who in San Juan, Puerto Rico, with the consent of three bishops, opened the First Continental Whore House, on August 4, 1526 — a memorable date, which today is celebrated as the *Día de la Raza,* because the girls who worked there had been brought from the peninsula, since the Indians, who had never practiced that trade, lacked the skills that you and I were acquainted with . . . isn't that right, sailor?" "In the history of America — which I consider mine, even though it bears the name of another — there were gentlemen of greater merit than Bartolomé Cornejo," said the Invisible Discoverer, offended. "I mean, after all, Sahagún, Motolinía, Fra Pedro de Gante . . ." "Who's arguing! And there was Simón Bolívar too!" The invisible simulacrum of the Invisible Christopher twitched invisibly. "I would rather that you not mention Simón Bolívar." "Excuse me!" said Doria. "I know that name gives you little pleasure, since he undid what you had accomplished." "But if you think about it, if the discovery of America had been directed by Henry of England, Simón Bolívar would have been named Smith or Brown . . ." "And by the same token, if Anne of Britanny had accepted your offer, instead of Spanish they'd be speaking some barbaric Morbihan dialect today." "Let me remind you," said Christopher, annoyed, "that before you went to battle in the service of Carlos V, you blissfully served King Francis I of France, who was his enemy. We Genovese know each other." "Sure, sure, sure, so well that we all know who is the admiral of battles and who the admiral of excursions. Where were your wars?" "Over there," said the navigator of Isabella and Ferdinand, pointing to the west. "Mine were here, in the Mediterranean. The difference is, while you used your lombard cannons to terrorize a few poor naked Indians with no more than a few rude spears that were quite ineffective against even one of our poorest ox-prods, I was for years the scourge of the Turk's fleet of ships." The conversation was turning sour. Andrea Doria changed the subject. "So how did things go for you in there?" (pointing to the great door of the basilica). "They turned me down." "Of course. You're a sailor and a Genoan." And elevating his tone he recited some verses from the *Divine Comedy: Ah, Genoans! People strange to all good custom, full of vice . . . Why are you not driven from the earth?* "They turned me down," repeated Christo-phoros in a sad voice. "You, Andrea, were a Grand Admiral and I only want to honor your memory as the memory of a Grand Admiral . . . I was also a Grand Admiral but because I wanted to be too grand I lost my stature as Grand Admiral." "You can console yourself with the knowledge that many statues have been raised in your honor throughout the world." "And not a one looks like me, because I came from mystery and I returned to mystery without leaving a painted or drawn trace of my human image. Besides, man does not live by statues alone. Today, because I was admired too much, some friends of mine

screwed me." "Of course. You're a sailor and a Genoan." "They
screwed me," repeated the other, almost in tears. Andrea Doria
put an invisible hand on his companion's invisible shoulder, and
said consolingly: "And who the hell got the idea that a sailor
could ever be canonized? There isn't a single sailor in the whole
assembly of saints! And that's because no sailor was born without sin." There was a long pause. The two Invisible Ones had no
more to say to each other. "Ciao, Columbus." "Ciao, Doria . . ."
And the man-who-was-condemned-to-be-a-man-like-all-the-
others remained in the precise spot in the plaza where, when
you looked at Bernini's columns, the one in front hid the other
three perfectly, so that all four appeared to be one. "An optical
illusion," he thought. "An optical illusion, like the West Indies
were for me. One day, on the coast of Cuba at a place I called the
Alpha-Omega, I said that one world ended there and another
began: another *Something,* another thing, that I myself could not
manage to make out . . . I had rent the veil of the unknown and
entered a new reality that surpassed my understanding, for there
are discoveries so momentous — though possible — that by their
very immensity they annihilate any mortal who dares to enter
them." And then the Invisible One recalled Seneca, whose
Medea had long been his inspiration; he had identified with
Tiphys, the helmsman of the Argonaut, in the well-known
verses that now seemed charged with prophetic significance:
*Tiphys dared to spread his venturous sail, the hidden lessons of the breezes
learning. . . . The seas subdued, the victor's law obeys, no vessel needs a
goddess's art in framing, nor oars in heroes' hands, the ocean taming: the
frailest craft now dares the roughest waves. Now, every bound removed,
new cities rise in lands remote, their ancient walls removing. . . . Where
men no more shall unknown courses measure, for round the world no
"farthest land" shall be . . .* Then, as the bells began to ring clearly,
that afternoon in Rome, he recited verses that seemed to allude
to his own destiny: *Tiphys, tamer of the deep, abandoned to an
untrained hand his vessel's helm. On a foreign shore, far from his native*

land he died; and now within a common tomb, 'midst unknown ghosts, he lies at rest. . . . And in the precise spot in the plaza where the four columns of the circular colonnades merged into one, the Invisible One evaporated into the air that enveloped and passed through him, and he became one with the transparent ether.

10 September 1978